ILLUSTRATED
NOVELS:
A NEW ART FORM
FOR A NEW AGE

They say a picture's worth a thousand words...and they're right.

As anyone who's seen a movie and then read the book it's based on

can tell you, every media has its own strengths, things it can do better

than any other form. And that's what Illustrated Novels bring:

the strengths of two different media—strong, elegant, cinematic prose

and detailed illustrations that speak volumes to the reader.

The power of prose
combined with the beauty
of rich illustrations.

ANNE McCAFFREY'S

THE UNICORN GIRL

AN ILLUSTRATED NOVEL

HarperPrism
A Division of HarperCollinsPublishers

HarperPrism

A Division of HarperCollins Publishers
10 East 53rd Street, New York, NY 10022

Designed by Michael Chatham

With sincere appreciation to Frank Curtis, Esq., for all his work on our behalf.

HarperPrism books may be purchased for educational, business, or sales promotional use. For information, please write: Special Markets Department, HarperCollins Publishers, 10 East 53rd Street, New York, NY 10022-5299.

ISBN: 0-06-105540-9

Printed in the United States of America
First Printing: December 1997

Visit HarperPrism on the World Wide Web at http://www.harpercollins.com

97 98 99 00 01 /RRD 10 9 8 7 6 5 4 3 2 1

ANNE McCAFFREY'S

THE UNICORN GIRL

AN ILLUSTRATED NOVEL

It is easy to look back, now, and see how, in a cosmos tainted by corruption and injustice, a symbol of hope and freedom for all appeared in the form of a lost soul.

For centuries, humanity had explored space and expanded its frontiers to other worlds, only to find itself alone in a galaxy seemingly empty of any other form of intelligent life. But when three isolated asteroid miners recovered a drifting lifepod in the rocky depths of an asteroid belt, all that changed. On that day, Calum Baird, Declan Gilloglie, and Rafik Nadezda pulled from that small, oddly-built craft a lifeform like none other they had ever encountered — a beautiful, young creature covered in a layer of fine white hair, her head adorned by an ivory horn like that of a Unicorn's.

The three named her Acorna and raised her as if she were their own child, learning that she possessed powerful natural abilities for healing. Eventually, she grew into a young adult and began to forge her own path, becoming a symbol of hope and salvation, first to the forgotten children of Kezdet, where oppressive child labor ruled the economy, and, then, to any throughout the galaxy who would open their eyes to her. Only Acorna's desire to find the world of her origin and, once again, walk among her own people kept her from finding complete happiness.

It is this search and Acorna's natural instinct to fight injustice and ease the suffering of others that urged her toward her destiny. In time, she became the stuff of myth and legend as those she met forced upon her the role of divinity. And, now, so many years later, who is to say she was not?

The tales in this volume chronicle Acorna's adventures as a protector, a healer, and a stranger, all chosen from a span of time before she located her homeworld. It is hoped this collection will be the first of many intended to keep her symbol alive and make certain she is not forgotten. For if we lose our legends and our myths, what, then, gentle reader, do we have left?

The Teller of Tales

ANNE McCAFFREY'S
THE UNICORN GIRL
TROUBLE
IN KEZDET

BY MICKEY ZUCKER REICHERT

LASHING AMBER AND SCARLET LIGHTS INVADED ACORNA'S SLEEP, and she rose from her bed with practiced caution. A toddler tumbled to the center of the mattress, mid-snore, snuggling deeper into the covers. A blond girl shifted sleepily, without seeming to notice Acorna's departure, and a six-year-old boy mumbled something indecipherable before flopping back into his previous position. Only three. Acorna smiled. Since she and her companions had rescued hundreds of Kezdet's younglings from a so-called "bonded labor," better designated slavery, the children had flocked to her in the dark of night, curling up beside the savior some called Lukia of the Light, others Epona, and still more, Sita Ram.

In the weeks that had passed, the children had rediscovered their crushed self-esteem in the rewards of living and working for Maganos Moon Mining, Ltd. They needed her physical presence less with each passing day. Someday, Calum, one of her three guardians, would discover the galaxy from which her lifepod, and her infant self, had drifted. Then, she would confront the decision of returning to the world from which she had come or remaining with the people she loved and the children she had helped to rescue. She did not know which she would choose;

but, until that moment came, she needed to work toward her charges' self-reliance.

Red and saffron patterns continued to strobe across the domed ceiling, mingling to orange where they overlapped. Acorna turned her attention to the source of the lights: her personal console. Understanding filtered through. Crimson indicated urgency, reinforced by the flashing; and the yellow lights demanded privacy. By convention, she must attend this matter personally and beyond the sight of prying eyes. *A private message for me?* Acorna cocked her head quizzically. A tangled cascade of silver curls glided across her left shoulder, fully revealing the short horn jutting from her forehead. She glanced one more time at the children. All three slept easily, eyes closed, chests rising and falling in gentle rhythm.

Joy still thrilled through Acorna at the sight of them, keeping past images at bay. She could never forget the scars, the advanced, treatable conditions left too long unattended, the dull eyes that had struggled desperately just to hold a ray of hope. So much had changed, but her memory would continue to haunt her as well as her young charges. The overseers of the mines; glass, match, and carpet factories; and brothels that had stolen the innocent hopes and dreams of Kezdet's children found it cheaper to replace the dead than to bother treating the ill and those they might infect.

For the millionth time, rage surged through Acorna. As she slipped into the chair in front of her console, she had to force open fingers clenched to stiff fists. As blood flow returned to her skin, restoring the pink tinge beneath her fine, white fur, she placed her hands on the console. Lacking a joint, her uniform-length fingers moved more clumsily than a human's across the buttons, but she easily typed in her personal code. The blinking lights disappeared, replaced by subdued letters:

FOR YOUR EYES ONLY. DO NOT PROCEED UNLESS ALONE.

Acorna narrowed her eyes at the redundancy of the warning. She tapped a random key, and more words flowed across the screen:

Lady Acorna

Congratulations on your many successes. The children on Kezdet were lucky for your interference. I would like to have assisted, but I have no powerful friends to protect me as you and many others do. I thought you would want to know that some children still remain trapped on Kezdet. They were unable to find you or the many who assisted, when the exodus occurred...

Acorna lowered her head. Although the Child Labor League had crashed through most of the schemes employed to prevent the children's escape, it seemed certain they had missed some well-hidden youngsters, those too ill to reach the space craft and others so broken-spirited or fearful that even the legends could not draw them to her. She had forced herself to revel in the thousands they had saved and to try to forget those few they might have overlooked. Yet, the worry haunted her in the

quiet moments before sleep. She dug her two-toed feet into the carpet. Whoever had sent the message might have knowledge that would allow Acorna access to some of those stragglers. Hope blazed, and her eyes devoured the remainder of the message:

...I know of a work group being exploited as thieves. Meet me in East Celtalan, at the lower entry of 14868 Celtdanna Way, in three days at 2000 hours. Knock twice slowly, three times quickly, then once slowly. My safety is in jeopardy, so you must come by yourself. If you do not, I cannot risk talking with you. If you do, I will give you the information you need to find and help those children. Do not speak of this to anyone, even those you most trust. The more who know, the greater my danger.

Acorna clamped her hands together as she scanned the last words, then watched as the message faded from the screen. The collapsing motion of the letters warned her that they would not return and she would find no record on back-up. *The address!* Terror jabbed through her, narrowing her pupils to vertical slits. Relieved memory followed. *14868 Celtdanna Way. Three days. 2000 hours.*

Acorna straightened her fingers, then

clenched them again. Calum had gone searching for her origins. Of her two other guardians, Rafik was preparing for his journey back to the Harakamian Estate as the newly chosen heir to his Uncle Hafiz's fortune and illegitimate business endeavors. Gill had his wedding plans to attend to. Acorna's thoughts slipped naturally to Gill's future brother-in-law, Pal Kendoro. Conjured images of the young man brought a touch of pink to her cheeks and an upward twitch to the corners of her broad lips. Her attraction to him would confound most. It seemed unlikely that creatures of such diverse origins could couple. Yet, aside from her flat chest, she seemed to match the form of an unusually tall and slender human female closely enough. It mattered to neither of them whether they could produce offspring. The children no longer enslaved on Kezdet had already become their own.

Acorna wished she had a way to contact the sender of the anonymous message, to reassure him or her that delivering the information to the proper people would assure, rather than damage, security. Any of her guardians, Pal, and his sisters, Judit and Mercy, could assist. The Kendoros had all suffered as Kezdet bond laborers before Gill's fiancée, Judit, had won her freedom with a scholarship and bought that of her brother and sister as well. Delszaki Li, financial backer of Maganos Mining Ltd. and long-time member of the Child Labor League, had enviable connections as well as a mind-boggling system of cameras and alarms that assured his own safety. Though shady in his dealings, Hafiz Harakamian had maintained the secrecy of his operation for decades. She could scarcely imagine a group more steeped in stealth or more competent with protections.

Acorna sighed, shaking her head and glancing toward the sleeping children again. The sender of the message had left her little choice. She would not violate the confidence of one who had risked so much to contact her, and she valued the lives of the children too much to sacrifice any of them. She would have to meet with the writer, alone, and convince him or her of the necessity of involving others.

Flying in the converted cargo hauler used to shuttle supplies for the rescued children, Pal Kendoro sat beside Acorna and behind the pilot. Pal studied his companion with obvious skepticism. "Explain to me again why we need to make this trip?"

Acorna flashed the half-smile that made her craziest notions irresistible to him, and her pupils widened to contented discs. "We need more clothes for the children."

"But," Pal protested feebly, running a

small hand through his straight, black hair, then letting it fall back into eyes the color and shape of almonds. "We bought enough to open three shops in anticipation."

"Now we know their real sizes. We can't have them running about in tight or baggy outfits." Acorna drew her own polysilk body-wrap more tightly around her, then smoothed her matching pants.

Pal's gaze followed her every movement. *Why not?*, his dark eyes seemed to ask, but his mouth never spoke the words. Instead, he sighed and sank back into his seat, content to follow where Acorna's wild and usually naively innocent intentions took him. "At least she took me with her," he mumbled beneath his breath, not quite softly enough for Acorna's acute hearing to miss. Her guardians had forced her to promise she would never travel to Kezdet alone. Her rescue of the children had ruined some two thirds of Kezdet's economy. Most factory owners and government officials feared Li's and Hafiz's power, but some might still harbor enough rage to dare open revenge.

Acorna patted Pal's hand, and he laced his

fingers through hers, his nut-brown skin a delicate contrast to her soft layer of ivory fur. Beneath the control console, she slipped off the sandals that never quite fit over her oddly-shaped feet.

The ship lurched on re-entry. A light flickered on the control panel, lending Pal's arms a greenish cast. Switches clicked beneath the pilot's steady hand, then the space craft settled back into a smooth motion, ruffled intermittently by turbulence in Kezdet's atmosphere.

Pal finally managed speech. "Couldn't we at least have left earlier in the day? By the time we get there, the shops'll be closed."

Acorna made a dismissive gesture. "It took me a while to get ready...and to figure out what we needed." She patted her pocket to indicate a list. "Many shops do their best business in the evening hours."

Pal grunted. Then silence settled over the converted cargo hauler as it idled down to Kezdet's dock and the pilot maneuvered the shuttle deftly into position. As soon as the doors swished open, Acorna dashed into the hangar. While Pal handled dock security and gave the

the delicate horn on her forehead. In the past, her guardians had made her cover the protuberance with turbans and scarves; but, on their last several trips to Kezdet, they had not bothered. Her appearance had become too familiar to too many to bother. Now, she lamented that she had not swathed it anyway. Pal would only need to follow the gawkers to find her.

At least, Acorna had deliberately worn pants, knowing from the start that she would have to ditch her companion. She winced at the thought, her pupils constricting. Though she felt guilty for lying to a man she respected as well as loved, for the moment rescuing children in bondage had to take precedence. She kept reminding herself of this even as she exited the hangar and trotted into Celtalan proper.

A study of the city map revealed the meeting site on the poorer eastside. Acorna had visited the area once, to cure a woman's hideously deforming facial birthmark as a favor to her brother. In the process of rescuing a child from the place, a brothel or "bonk-shop" as the children called it, she had barely managed, with Gill's help, to fight her

pilot instructions, she swiftly lost herself in the twists and turns of the station. Dockworkers in coveralls mingled with merchants and businessmen awaiting transportation. Many paused to stare at the remarkably slim giant of a young woman who darted and dodged between patrons, silvery hair streaming around

way free. This further narrowed her silvery pupils, yet she did not slacken her pace. She galloped onto the Riverwalk, Celtalan's glory of city planning. Entering the park, she quickened her pace, unable to suppress her excitement at the mingled perfume of fresh, damp grasses, budding flowers, and purified water. The high-pitched tinkle of tiny, manufactured waterfalls and the sweet laughter of lovers snuggled in half-size gazebos added beauty to the rapidly receding colors of the gardens.

Dodging pedestrians and low-flying skimmers grew from necessity to rarity as Acorna ran eastward. Soon, manicured gardens gave way to spillage, occasional flowers intermingled with choking vines and weeds. Even these disappeared beneath her pounding feet, the hard-packed ground that followed still a pleasure. Once before, she had run this way; but this time she had prepared herself for the fetid, oily waters that had not yet reached the purification centers westward. She knew the river bridge would carry her safely over the murky water and onto a paved road lined with commercial stands. Deliberately, she avoided it, lurching northward toward a congested cluster of hovels. Up a mossy hill she flew, heart pounding from more than the anticipation of meeting with the anonymous sender. Legs pumping, the green and brown expanse scrolling beneath her feet, the wind dancing through her hair; these things seemed natural

in a way Maganos did not, though she had helped to create it. Compared with plants naturally grown, hydroponics seemed contrived, no matter how carefully balanced the flora and soil nutrients. Even tainted with filth, the air planetside seemed fresher, erratically twined with a vast spectrum of scents.

As Acorna reached the base of the hill, she slowed her gait. Gathering her legs and equilibrium, she vaulted over the dusky, foul-smelling river, landing on the far bank with a gentle thump that tingled through her ankles. Small footsteps pounded through a nearby alley, and the sheeting sound of fabric scraping brick reached her ears from the opposite direction. Standing amid primitive packed earth pathways that made East Celtalan seem like a whole different world, she collected her bearings. The last time she came here, she had ridden in a skimmer, and she labored to combine remembered details with her study of the map.

At length, Acorna plotted her route. Pal had taught her to avoid alleyways in favor of well-lit streets, but she found the latter too scarce to wholly accommodate her. Dusk settled over sagging cottages and the threadways that separated them, hiding the dirt but not the sagging constructions. The few people she passed shied away from her strange appearance, apparently assessing her differences as deformities or worrying for the sanity of one who chose to travel the back streets of

14

the bad-side alone. She had spent most of her life on a space craft, maturing to adulthood in less than four years and assisting her three guardians with mining asteroids. It never occurred to her to worry for her safety simply because of the location she had chosen to walk, thus she showed none of the natural fear that draws predators on dark city streets.

Acorna found the rough stretches of pavement, interrupted by patches of shattered rock and slime, that defined Celtdanna Way. She followed the few buildings with numbers toward 14868. The closer she drew, the more familiar the area became, until she found herself standing in front of the same basement entrance to the precise dwelling where she had healed the port-wine birthmark. Moss coated the surface, so thick she could not determine the material of its construction. Grime caked the windows, hiding the goings-on inside. Carefully, Acorna clambered down the slippery steps and tapped the appropriate pattern on the door: two slow, three rapid, and one slow.

A spy hole clicked, but the warped glass revealed nothing to Acorna. Then, the panel eased open a crack. A head edged partway through, revealing smooth brown skin, clean hair without a hint of gray that contrasted starkly with the filth of her surroundings, and a dark eye as hard and cold as a diamond chip.

The stranger's gaze flickered over Acorna, and a softening gleam entered it. A meaty arm snaked through the opening and ushered her inside.

Acorna hesitated. The last time she had visited this house, men had seized her; but things had changed much since she had first come to Kezdet. This woman looked harmless enough, and her note had sounded fearful.

"Come in," the woman whispered. "Please." Her hand trembled. "The longer you stand out there, the more likely someone will see you."

For the children, Acorna reminded herself, heading toward the door.

The crack broadened to admit Acorna into a dimly lit hallway. Only then she received a full view of the woman as she closed the door behind them and dropped the bolt into place. Tall and plump, she wore a colorful kameez embroidered gold along each seam, and a ring adorned nearly every finger. Her movements revealed glimmering anklets occasionally sparkling beneath the hem. Her perfume wafted through the area, cloyingly sweet. She waited several moments, ear pressed to the door. Apparently satisfied, she turned her attention fully and suddenly on Acorna.

The change startled Acorna further into silence.

"Thank you for coming," the woman said graciously. "I apologize for the secrecy. I do hope you haven't mentioned this meeting to anyone."

Acorna swallowed and nodded confirmation.

The woman did not wait for Acorna to speak before ushering her toward the first room on the right hand side. Acorna barely managed a glance, her pupils shrinking against the darkness; but the hallway appeared to sport an unusual number of rooms on both sides before tapering into unbroken darkness.

Following the woman's gesture, Acorna stepped into a bare room containing, at first glance, nothing. Whitewashed walls bore nicks, scars, and smudges, but seemed otherwise generally clean. Vents smaller than Acorna's fist entered the ceiling at each far corner, probably an air purification system or air conditioning conduits. An irregularity near the superior edge of the farthest wall caught her attention. It appeared to be a dark rectangle, its long sides parallel to the floor. A moment later, she recognized it as the lower edge of a window. An incompetent or unconventional builder had placed it inappropriately low so that, while most of it occupied the room above, a tiny portion opened here. More likely, Acorna supposed, the owner could not afford separate windows for both levels and so had found a way to combine them.

While Acorna contemplated the oddity, the door slammed suddenly behind her. The snap of the lock reverberated through the room.

Acorna whirled. "Hey!" she shouted, giving the door a sharp rap with her foot. "What's going on?"

The lock clicked again, and the door winched back open. The same woman stood there, eyes wide and expression apologetic. "I'm so sorry. I didn't mean to startle you. I thought I told you I was bringing the woman who needs to talk to you." She glanced about quickly, as if terrified someone might overhear, then continued in a whisper. "About the children, I mean. Security. I'm trying to keep you both safe."

Feeling silly, Acorna lowered her foot to the floor. "No, you didn't tell me."

"Here." Groping into the darkness, the woman emerged with a glass of dark and remarkably pulpy madigadi juice. She thrust it into Acorna's hand. "Something to drink while you're waiting, sweetie." Without another word, she swept the door shut and slammed the tumblers to lock again.

This time the action did not startle Acorna, and it occurred to her that the latching posed her no danger. She was inside, not out, and so should be able to work the lock without a key. Gliding nearer to the door, she sought a mechanism to open it; but the frayed rope pulley that

dangled where the doorknob should sit provided minimal purchase. It would function well enough that she could open the door when unlocked, yet would prove worthless in the circumstances in which she found herself now. *Strange arrangement. Why?*

Before Acorna could ponder long, a bead of liquid oozed down her forehead, followed by a second. The gentle tickle of its spiral passage along her hair revealed its origin as her horn. Immediately, she turned her attention to the cup in her hand. The juice looked no different then before, yet experience told her it had to contain poison. Before she could think to do anything different, she plunged her horn into the liquid, splashing droplets to the bare stone floor. A moment later, she withdrew, the horn now dribbling only juice and the drink fully purified. Absently, she sipped it, tossing another glance around the room. It appeared no different than before, an unadorned, unfurnished box with only the vents, the door and the misplaced window to break the monotony of its chalky walls.

Accustomed to months at a time aboard an overcrowded mining vessel, Acorna did not find the confinement unusually bothersome. The lack of objects to occupy her attention disturbed her more. She sat cautiously on the floor, the cold of the stonework seeping through her pants, and took swallows of slightly sour, but no longer poisoned, juice. *I'll have to warn the woman I'm meeting to watch what she consumes. Apparently, someone wants to prevent our conference.* Finishing the drink, she set the cup on the floor beside her.

For several minutes longer, Acorna remained alone with her thoughts. She wondered if Pal could forgive her and if he would ever trust her again. She winced at the deeper realization of the horrible trick she had played on him. He would worry about her disappearance, every moment of wondering a torment. She thought of the three gentle miners who had raised her and hoped Pal had not yet sent messages that would distress them as well. Then, her mind turned to the children, a smile bowing her lips without specific intent. The lengthy list of necessary duties on Maganos, Kezdet's primary satellite, filled several more minutes of waiting.

Finally, after what seemed like at least an hour, Acorna rose and paced a few steps, feet clacking against stone. Memory of her run through the park gradually turned confinement into an intolerable burden. She paced the length of the room, only then noticing a change in the rectangle of window. Someone had cleared away a ragged peephole, scratched through layers of grime that plated the outside pane.

Acorna reached up an arm, but could not catch the lower ledge of plastic trim surrounding the glass. Bouncing did not solve the problem. She backed to the door but found the space to the window inadequate for a running leap. It seemed rude to hammer on the door a second time. Yet, if someone had harmed the woman who led her here before she could fetch the sender of the message, no one would know Acorna had become trapped here. She cocked a foot for a hefty kick, when suddenly, her mind registered a change in the character of the air. The vents hissed like angry snakes, and trickles of deadly carbon monoxide swirled into the room.

Didi Badini flopped her ample bottom onto a flowered divan in the lush, second story of her otherwise dismal-appearing brothel. Her eyes traveled from the dark and silent vid-screen, to the computer-duplicated masterpieces hung in perfect rows, to the thickly cushioned chair across from her current position. Decorative glass bowls containing buds and multicolored candies sat in tasteful displays on a broad table, and a lidded vase held more than two dozen happy-sticks.

The door burst open, and Kisla Manjari stormed into the room, mouse-brown hair streaming and elfin features pinched. "You should have seen that deformed bitch! Stuck that point on her head in the juice, then drank it like pure damned Kyllian honey!"

Didi Badini made a brisk gesture.

In response, Kisla hooked the edge of the door with a foot and awkwardly yanked it closed, talking the whole while. "Didn't touch her. Not even a snore. And there was enough in there to kill three—"

"That's enough," Didi Badini said, waving a fleshy, brown arm. "The gas will handle her."

"Maybe," Kisla huffed, jerking at the shirt that dangled from her skeletal body like a dress. "She's a monster, that creature. May take a religious ceremony to destroy her."

"Nonsense." Didi Badini yanked the cord that controlled the flood of carbon monoxide into the Uncooperatives' Room, now occupied by Acorna. Many times, she had filled that same area with sleeping gases to control children until she could train them to service the brothel's clients. "Her metabolism may not work like ours, or perhaps the claims about that healing horn are not so exaggerated as I once believed. But she is mortal. I'm certain of it."

Kisla released a noncommittal snort. Her late father, the Baron, had virtually ruled Kezdet until Acorna revealed him as the notorious Piper, the man responsible for maintaining the child-bond-labor situation that fueled Kezdet's economy. The revelation had driven him to murder her mother before taking his own life. In the process, all of Kezdet had learned that she, herself, was the product of a brothel pregnancy, not the natural, pureblooded royalty she and her father had always believed. To add insult to injury, Acorna and her companions had commandeered Kisla's personal fleet of ships to transport the ragged and filthy urchins to Maganos Moon Base. Kisla's eyes, as piercing as her father's, gleamed with a deadly, spiteful rage that only Acorna's death or torture would satisfy.

The memory sparked Didi Badini's own hatred. Left with only willing adult prostitutes to fill the bedrooms of her brothel, she had lost many of her highest paying customers, those who trusted her to cater to their appetites

for children, brutality, or both. Throughout Kezdet, the Didis and their guild suffered for the lack of enslaved children Acorna and the Child Labor League had created. Broken, too, was her link to Kezdet's government, leaving only Kisla, who had lost her own status by her mother's confession.

"Let's go look," Kisla demanded, heading back out the door before Didi Badini could answer.

Releasing the lever, the Didi followed Kisla out the front door, jogging after her anorexic form as she headed to the window. The odd symmetry of the fixture bothered her every time she saw it, but it suited the clients who wished to examine her newest goods without needing to fend off kicks and punches. She found Kisla crouched at the improvised peek hole and hurried to the younger woman's side, just as Kisla rose, slammed her fist against the brick work and rounded on Didi Badini. "You are not going to believe this."

Dropping to one knee, Didi Badini took over Kisla's place, the manner and words of the baron's daughter cueing her to expect the worst. Even before her eyes adjusted to the light, she discerned Acorna's silver form from the dank interior. The oddity stood beneath one of the vents, horn leveled toward it like a lance seeking a target. Didi Badini's fingers balled to bloodless fists. "Impossible," she muttered, rage boiling into an unsortable tempest. That horn.

"You saw it. I saw it." Kisla said, her voice a growl. "She's unkillable."

Didi Badini dropped to her haunches, saying nothing.

"She's unkillable," Kisla repeated.

Didi Badini shook her head. "No. If she were, her friends would not spend so much time and effort protecting her." Her features crinkled, breaking creases in the thick layer of facial powder. "And we know for certain that she can be contained."

Kisla turned the Didi a questioning look. "Are you thinking…"

"I'm thinking," Didi Badini finished quietly, "that a lot of my old clients might find one of her appearance…" She laid her palms together. "…entertaining."

"You wouldn't." Kisla's grin seemed to encompass her entire face.

"Eventually, I'll have one of the…um… less gentle types remove that horn. It'll bring good money, too."

"The horn?"

"Powdered unicorn horn," she prompted.

Kisla nodded, finally dredging the legends from her memory. "Aphrodisiac."

"Believe me," Didi Badini finished. "I'll definitely find a buyer."

As darkness washed over the crudely cleaned spot on the brothel's window, turning Acorna's world to pitch, she slumped wearily to the floor. The doors and walls bore the scars of her kicks, though she had accomplished nothing more than gouging splinters into her toes. The room stank from residual carbon monoxide; enough had oozed through the vents to overwhelm the purifying capacity of her horn. Though not enough to kill her, the dregs bothered the sensitive membranes of her mouth, nose, and ears. Exhausted by her attempts to escape, she drifted into sleep.

Pal paced frantically along the hangar, awaiting the fastest space craft from the Maganos Moon Base to arrive. *Why would she do this? Why, oh why?* His own search for Acorna had led him to the grungiest, dirtiest part of the eastside, then had dead-ended. The people he approached ran from him, and occasionally, he heard stealthy movements: a footstep, a cough, the scrape of fabric against stone, or the rasp of a drawn knife. Aware that losing his own life to street thugs or gangs would do Acorna no good, he had summoned Gill and Rafik from the base, as well as contacting his former employer, Delszaki Li. If the head of a multibillion credit financial and industrial empire and his net of information could not locate Acorna, then she was unfindable. And

21

Gill and Rafik would have the muscle-power and know-how to help him free her from danger.

Why, oh why? Pal's stride increased, already a quick, jerky movement that drew every nearby eye. A tear dribbled down his cheek. Recognition of it brought more, until a relentless, warm cascade ran along every part of his face. The urge to dash back to where Acorna's trail had grown cold seized him. He found himself halfway toward the door before common sense intervened. For several moments, he stood, locked in place, unable to move in any direction. *Wait for Gill and Rafik,* he admonished himself. *You can't do anything without them.* Yet, a deeper, darker corner of his mind told him that every moment alone placed Acorna further into danger. *Why, oh why, oh why?*

❀ ❀ ❀

A light touch awakened Acorna. She sprang to her feet, spinning to face this new threat. A child scrambled from the sudden movement, dropping into a defensive crouch. "Don't hurt me, Sita Ram. Please, don't hurt me." Wide brown eyes peeked from beneath protective fingers, and slender, dirt-streaked limbs jutted from a tattered kameez. Though hair hung shaggily to the young-ster's shoulders, she believed he was a boy, about ten years old. "I wouldn't ever harm you," Acorna assured him. "You just startled me."

The boy lowered his arms. "I'm called Sanga, Sita Ram." He glanced at the door, then his attention drifted to the window.

Acorna followed his gaze. Someone had cut away the filthy glass in a rectangle that exactly matched the portion built below the upper story. A knotted and grimy rope dangled from the outside.

Footsteps thumped outside the door. Sanga pranced a hysterical circle. "Quick, Sita Ram. Out! Out!" He jerked a thumb toward the window.

"You first, Sanga," Acorna insisted as she took several steps in the proper direction.

"No, please." Sanga seized her arm, as if to drag her outside. He seemed impossibly small to direct her seven foot frame.

The door rattled.

"I won't leave ahead of you. Don't argue. Just go!" The urgency of Sanga's voice sent Acorna dashing to obey. She scrambled up the rope, jamming her head through the opening. The space proved smaller than she expected. Her shoulders wedged between the upper surface of glass and the trim. Her feet raked the wall beneath, scrambling for purchase. She wriggled, wood and dull-edged glass gouging furrows from flesh. Then, several small hands gripped both of her arms, tugging even as she writhed toward them. Pain screamed through her arms and neck, and it felt as if her collarbones would shatter. She heard the door behind her creak as her shoulders popped through, the rest of her body following like a baby gliding from the womb. A shout of frustration reverberated through the brothel room, then Sanga started scuttling through the hole behind her.

Suddenly, the boy's body jerked backward. "They got me," he hissed, desperation raising his voice an octave. Small figures dived for his disappearing arms and head. Closer, Acorna caught his left forearm. His fingers entwined around her wrist, and his other hand flailed for support. She grabbed that, also, planting her feet and tugging with all her strength. She met resistance like stone, and her singly-jointed fingers began to slip. Even as they did, Sanga's grip tightened defensively.

A childish female shout rang out behind her. "Pull!"

"Oh, don't give up." A slight figure paced frantically on the broken cobbles.

"Hold on, Sanga," a boy's voice followed from nearby, and another pair of hands gripped Sanga's arms.

Sanga grunted in pain, eyes clamped closed and cheeks red with strain. His hold slipped, shifting, and Acorna felt herself losing hers, as well. With a desperate effort, she threw all her strength into one abrupt yank, just as the boy assisting did the same. Sanga flew free. Their momentum toppled Acorna. She landed on her back, dirt smearing her bodywrap and pants, jagged edges of stone stamping bruises along her back. A vile string of swear words echoed through the room below.

"Oh, no," a young girl slurred. "We killed Lukia."

Small hands tugged at Acorna, helping her to stand. Sanga beckoned as he darted down a side street with two others. Acorna clasped a hand from each of her remaining benefactors, trotting after the disappearing children. The pudgy, sticky fingers in her left fist belonged to a girl no older than six with coffee-colored skin and sleek black hair that fell to her shoulders. The other sported small breasts on an otherwise pre-adolescent figure, probably twelve or thirteen years old. Her long, narrow face could have looked pretty with several centimeters more depth and some thickness and contour to the lips. Blond hair perched like a fuzzy ball atop her head, heightening the disproportion of her features.

They ran along several streets, cutting through narrow, dark alleyways at irregular intervals. A half-moon added a glaze to an otherwise dreary landscape, revealing discarded electronics, scraps of cardboard and misplaced cobbles. Acorna skirted these, cautious for the steps of her new companions as well. The younger girl panted, and her weight became a progressively more noticeable strain on Acorna's arm. Just as she considered carrying the child, Sanga and his companions came to a stop on a quiet, empty thoroughfare. He bounced to a sitting position on a cracked wooden crate, the young girl and one of the ones who had run ahead, joining him; the

others leaning against a filthy brick building with boarded windows.

Now, Acorna studied all of them. In addition to Sanga and the two girls, she discovered two more boys. One was tall and lanky, with close-cropped red hair and dark eyes that never seemed still. The other was shorter and younger, perhaps nine, dressed in sagging, tattered britches, a too-small kameez, and a belt wrapped twice around his waist.

Sanga introduced them quickly, indicating the youngest boy first. "Zathan." He inclined his head toward the girl still catching her breath, "Charlas," then toward the other girl, "Hannoh." He tapped the tallest boy last. "We call him Red, of course."

Acorna nodded a greeting to each, her smile wide and her pupils round as suns. "Thank you for saving me."

"Lady Epona," Zathan said. "You've done too much good for us to act otherwise."

Hannoh added, "We saw you going into that awful place." She shivered, her knowledge of it undoubtedly first hand. "We couldn't let them hurt you."

"Lukia of the Light," Charlas corrected, wheezing out another of the names the anxious children had used for the legendary horned healer-woman who would rescue them from their travails. From that, Acorna realized she dealt with an oddly mixed group. What the

children called her, she had discovered, mostly depended upon whether they had been enslaved in the mines, factories, or brothels.

Sanga leapt in, obviously trying to offset an argument over semantics. "What were you doing in Didi Badini's bonk-shop?"

Acorna shuffled her bare feet, kicking up a cloud of dust. "She promised me information about…" Urgency finally abated enough for her to put together the obvious. "…you, it appears." She patted Charlas' arm. "But I'd trust the information you give me much more."

"Can you really heal things?" Charlas blurted, earning a stern look from Hannoh.

"Yeah." Zathan hefted a sandaled foot, balancing it on the crate. "Can you fix this?" The flesh on the upper surface of his foot swirled into ghoulish patterns that scarcely resembled normal skin. Only his second and third toes remained recognizable, the others melted into the mass. Surely, this had come of spilling something molten in one of Kezdet's factories, mostly likely glass. Blue eyes rolled to Acorna's face, then shyly flitted away. She saw a tiny sparkle of hope.

Leaning over, Acorna touched her horn to Zathan's foot. Exhausted from excitement, long hours and cleansing poisons, she nearly succumbed to a wave of dizziness. Unaware of her discomfort, the children huddled around boy and healer as the flesh smoothed to a featureless expanse, then slowly returned to its normal conformation. Gasps escaped the children, followed by a silence so intense it seemed evil to break it.

Finally, Zathan did so. "Th-thank you," he managed, eyes never leaving his foot. "Thank you!" he shouted again suddenly, head thrown back in euphoric triumph. He ran a hand over his foot, tracing every line with a finger, then weaving in and out between his toes. "Thank you, thank you, thank you."

Hannoh grinned. "There are others who could use your help, if you can spare it, Lady."

"Even the Dodger hisself," Charlas said excitedly, abruptly silenced by warning glares from her companions.

"Dodger?" Acorna repeated.

The children exchanged glances. "It's safe to tell *her*," Sanga insisted, and nods slowly circumnavigated the group. When no one else volunteered an explanation, Sanga took the initiative again, "Some of us escaped from the mines and other places." He coughed once, with the deep rattle Acorna recognized in those who had spent years inhaling coal dust or guano. Once he finished speaking, she promised herself, she would heal him, too. "Others got tossed out on the streets because of sickness or accidents, left for dead." He glanced toward Zathan who still studied his foot as if incapable of believing it whole.

Charlas' hands slid toward her privates, and Acorna suspected she had unwittingly revealed that she had caught something in one of Kezdet's brothels. Rage flared at the idea of one so young abused by perverts without a shred of human decency.

Oblivious to the many directions of Acorna's thoughts, Sanga coughed again, then continued. "Turns out it's usually cheaper to buy new healthy workers than help the old ones get better."

Though Acorna had heard the same from her guardians and the rescued children, it still enraged her.

"Anyways," Red interrupted, his first words since Acorna came among them. "Most kids die on the streets, 'cept those of us lucky 'nough to meet up with Dodger. He tooked us in, helps take care of what's wrong and makes us work together to get food and clothes and stuff."

Acorna believed she had the last piece of the puzzle. "Then he makes you steal for him."

"He don't make us," Charlas defended.

Sanga shrugged. "It's not as if—" he started, interrupted by the sound of pounding feet and voices.

A call followed, loud and full of desperate need, "Acooorna!" She recognized Pal's voice.

"It's…," Acorna trailed off as the children scattered into the alley's depths. "Wait! Come back! It's safe!"

The small forms vanished into the darkness as Pal, Rafik, and Gill rounded the corner.

"A—" Gill started, then stopped as he caught sight of her. "There she is!"

Pal rushed to Acorna, catching her into an embrace that she warmly returned. Rafik took a harsh position, hands on hips, dark eyes trained on Acorna; but that could not fully hide the relief that filled his expression. Gill whooped, his red hair an unruly mop and his huge, sturdy form familiar and comforting.

"You're all right," Pal said, grip tightening around her. "Thank goodness, you're all right."

Acorna struggled free, silver eyes scanning the alleyway for some sign of the children. "Sanga, Charlas, Hannoh, come back." No movement followed her plea, no sign any of them had heard or obeyed. "Please. Red, Zathan. They won't hurt you." Still, no one replied. No child reappeared.

Tears filled Acorna's eyes. Clearly, the children would not return.

Pal gripped her arms, flicking a tear from her lashes. "What's going on, Acorna?" His face twisted as he shared an anguish he did not yet understand. "What happened? Why did you run from me?"

Rafik made a crisp gesture over his shoulder. "Explanations in the skimmer. A dark alley on the worst side of town is not a wise place for a chat."

Acorna glanced around one more time, finding no sign the children had ever existed. Allowing Gill and Pal to each take an arm, she followed Rafik to a skimmer parked on the main avenue. She recognized the driver from his assistance with freeing the children in the past. It was his sister's face that Acorna had healed in the brothel. "Pedir," she said, managing a smile.

The driver returned a brisk salute as Acorna and the men scrambled into the skimmer behind him. As it lifted from the ground and settled into normal flying pattern, Rafik rounded on Acorna. "You did a very dangerous and foolish thing, not to mention hurting and worrying Pal."

Acorna lowered her head, silver curls falling softly around her face. "I know," she said in a small voice, then raised her head imbued with sudden courage. "But I found a group of children who escaped bonded labor only to be enslaved as thieves, performing the dirty work of a man they call the Dodger."

Rafik's lids shot up, but he did not express his surprise. "A worthy cause," he admitted, "but not worth your life, Acorna. We will help you free these children, just as we did the others. But we will work together."

He looked directly into Acorna's eyes. "Together, agreed?"

Acorna nodded. She deserved the severity and the lecture. "Agreed," she said.

Gill and Pal relaxed visibly.

Once safely in Delszaki Li's compound, Rafik's diatribe continued, now joined by Li, Hafiz, and Pal. They sat around a dining room table that could have seated thirty, feasting on smoked game imported from three planets, aromatic cheeses, and crisp fruits and vegetables that ranged from deep green leaves to purple, orange, and red madigadis. As usual, Acorna ate only flora, stuffing her mouth with some of the most flavorful plants and sweetest fruits she had ever tasted.

"...and furthermore," droned the heir to the Harakamian empire, "you placed all of us in

danger by sending us racing to this stink hole of a planet that's already the sewer of the galaxy…" Catching himself, he glanced apologetically at Li, "No offense intended."

Seated in his hover-chair, Li dismissed the need for regret with a tolerant wave of his wrinkled, veiny left hand. "Some might say I own the planet, but they would be wrong."

"Not very," Pal mumbled, not quite inaudibly.

Rafik lowered a forkful of meat. "Where was I?"

Gill winked at Acorna. "Hopefully, toward the end of a sermon you started two hours ago." He added so that only Acorna, beside him, could hear, "And to which we all stopped listening one and half hours ago." He squeezed Acorna's leg beneath the table to indicate that, while he believed Rafik had run on interminably, he still agreed with his partner's reasoning.

Rafik stuffed the morsel into his mouth, making a noncommittal noise as he chewed.

At Acorna's other hand, Pal cleared his throat. "If we're all done scolding Acorna, now, I'd really like to hear about the children."

Gill nodded vigorously.

As the onus to speak finally fell on her, Acorna realized how exhausted she had become. She fought drooping eyelids as she detailed her experiences in Kezdet's eastside, including her escape from Didi Badini and the conversation with Sanga and the other children in the roadway. As Acorna reached the point where their sudden presences had frightened the boys and girls away, fatigue became a constant, heavy presence she could no longer ignore. "Now, if you'll excuse me, I have to get some sleep."

Pal leapt to his feet, steering Acorna to the bedroom she had used during their previous stay. Before joining Acorna on Maganos, he had served as Li's personal assistant for many years, tending to the old man's security and other affairs. Now, his younger sister, Mercy, filled that role; but he still knew his way around and still acted as if the mansion could not function in his absence.

With a mumbled "good night," Acorna crawled into her bed on top of the covers and drifted almost immediately to sleep.

When Pal Kendoro returned to the dining room, he found it empty aside from servants clearing dishes. Several gave him happy waves; even those secretly in the employ of the Guardians of the Peace, Kezdet's corrupt police force; and had gotten along well with him when he had tended the Li affairs. Though pleased with his sister's work as well, they surely missed him as much as he did them.

One approached, his thick lips parted in a grin that revealed his large teeth. He clapped a

massive hand onto Pal's arm. "Hey, Pal-oh. Long time."

"A couple months, only," Pal corrected. "Where are the others?"

"Mr. Li and his guests are taking tea in the downstairs study. They said to steer you there."

"Consider me steered." Pal spread his arms like skimmer wings. "Thanks, Gregori."

The servant nodded acknowledgment, then returned to his work while Pal ambled through the south door toward the downstairs study. Fatigue caught up to him as well, and he yawned as he trod the spotless carpet. At length, he reached the door and tapped quietly so as not to disturb any conversation taking place inside.

The door glided open to reveal Gill standing in the doorway. The colossal asteroid miner stepped aside and gestured Pal into the room. Li floated in his specially equipped hover-chair, the victim of a wasting neuromuscular disease that had rendered his legs and right arm all but useless. That he had remained in charge of his financial empire for fifteen years after his enemies had predicted his speedy demise was a testament not only to his strength but to his intelligence and stubborn will to do so much more than just survive. Pride twinged through Pal. Once a childhood bonded laborer, he had become the arms, legs, and eyes, of this great man. Though he had

passed the task on to his sister, it had instilled in him an enormous quantity of dignity and self-respect, a faith in himself that he had once believed crushed beyond resurrection. He owed Delszaki Li much more than the kind old man would ever understand.

Hafiz Harakamian sprawled across most of the couch, while Rafik accepted the single remaining cushion, mouth tight and arms folded across his chest. With his defensive stance and his elegant features taut, he bore the same aura of dangerous wariness that seemed always to define his uncle. Gill returned to a plush recliner, leaving one exactly like it for Pal. The young man closed the door behind him, then perched on the only open seat. "What's going on?"

Gill explained. "We're discussing what to do about Acorna's little mishap."

"Giant," Rafik corrected.

Gill smiled. "Giant mishap."

"Catastrophe," Rafik revised again.

"Colossal, planet-shattering, appalling, re-pulsive tragedy," Gill amended.

Now, it was Rafik's turn to smile. "Thank you."

"You're welcome."

Ignoring the exchange, Li took up where the previous conversation had left off.
"Clever man. Take unwanted children. Win trust by treating and feeding. Then use to steal for him."

"Evil man," Rafik inserted, either tired or bold enough to alter even the words of the mansion's owner.

Hafiz grunted. Pal could not help wondering if the crooked head of Harakamian house wished he had thought of the scheme first.

Gill cleared his throat. "Perhaps I'm thinking with the quote, 'Viking-ancestor part of what you laughingly refer to as my brain' unquote, again, but…" He trailed off, as if recalling the familiar insult had caused him to forget his original point. "…evil?"

Rafik examined his friend as if he had transformed into a Gheredian slime-spider in front of his eyes. "What would you call a man who manipulates traumatized, desperately needy children into stealing for him?"

"Shady." Gill ran a hand through his stiff, red beard. "In that, he's not alone on this planet." He added with pointed caution, "He's not even alone in this room."

Hafiz took no obvious offense. In fact, wrinkles of amusement touched his cheeks and eyes.

"But," Gill said. "Whatever his motives, at least he found ways to tend their wounds and afflictions, which is more than I can say for any of the so-called bosses at the mines and factories. And to feed them. Alone on the streets, those children would have starved or succumbed to the slow agony of their diseases."

Rafik turned Gill a hard stare, his slender, brown fingers tensed like claws. "By the Three Prophets! You're suggesting we allow this to continue?" He shook his head. "Declan Giloglie the Third, you have officially taken leave of your simple, barbarian senses."

Pal's attention shifted naturally back to Gill, who took the indignity in commendable stride.

"I'm not saying we put this Dodger guy on our charity list." Gill dropped his hands to his lap, leaning toward the couch. "I'm just saying maybe we shouldn't place him in the same category as a mass murderer. Or even a factory owner."

Pal could see both sides. "Maybe it's better to win this guy over, rather than put him out of business."

"What!" Rafik roared. Even Li's thin, black brows rose as all attention shifted to Pal.

"Hear me out." Pal opened his palms. "The Dodger brings the escapees and outcasts together. If we paid him enough for each child, they become more valuable as a salable commodity than for his own personal use." He spread his hands, indicating the rest should seem obvious. "A steady supply of Kezdet's remaining bond laborers. If he's as good a collector as he seems, he might be able to help liberate any of Kezdet's children still enslaved, not to mention any new children illegally sold into service."

Silence followed, interspersed with thoughtful nods.

"Not bad," Li and Hafiz said, almost simultaneously. The similarities between a generous, honest businessman and an unethical one never ceased to amaze Pal.

Even Rafik made conciliatory gestures with his hands. Gill offered Pal Kendoro a wink that expressed thanks. Eventually, he probably would have made the same point; but having someone better known for education and brains on his side had helped immensely.

"All we have to do, then," Li said, "is find and talk to this Dodger."

Hafiz loosed a soft huff, his way of proclaiming *impossible* a plan that Li had boiled down to its simplest, though irresolvable, elements. "Of course, you know how and where to find him."

"No clue," Li admitted in a flat tone that implied it was only a matter of time and a bit of effort, well within his capabilities. Pal Kendoro knew his one-time charge too well. Li believed everything was within his capabilities, which did not necessarily mean that this, or anything else, truly was. A corporate leader who did not see himself as invincible and see everything as within his grasp seldom went far, and Li had become the richest man on Kezdet. "But," he continued. "We will find him."

Pal Kendoro nodded gingerly. In the last

decade, he had found many things for Delszaki Li that others would have believed unattainable.

Rafik spoke the words on Pal's mind. "Acorna said he gathered escapees as well as cast outs. I doubt we're the only ones looking for him."

"But," Li turned his hover-chair toward both members of the Harakamian empire. "The difference: we will succeed."

Pal Kendoro ran through lists of names until dryness burned his eyes and rendered the letters incomprehensible. His vid screen became a blur of amber against the familiar "eye-gentle" green-gray. With a sigh that blended exhaustion with frustration, he threw himself back in the chair. It gave gently, bouncing him lightly into this new reclining position, its sand-filled stretch-synthetic cushion molding perfectly to the contours of his body. Too many. Can't sort this. Every input he attempted generated thousands of names or none at all. One thing seemed certain. They knew too little about this Dodger character for technology to assist in the search.

Groaning, Pal leaned forward and slumped against the input board. Buttons clicked beneath the pressure, followed by error beeps of varying pitches, intensities, and durations. Music. Pal laughed as the idea ran through his head in that giddy, ludicrously hopeful manner that can only come from mind-altering substances or, as in this case, from intense weariness. He hoped Gill, Rafik, and Hafiz fared better.

Li's regular, generous donations to the vacation and retirement funds of Kezdet's Guardians of the Peace assured that they raided Didi Badini's brothel, though they did wait until morning to avoid embarrassing certain officials who might have spent the night as guests. From the dingy, grubby streets of East Celtalan, Gill and Rafik watched as they paraded scantily clad women onto the shoulder of the broken street. Most shivered in the cooler, morning air; accustomed to Kezdet's daily heat, they seemed to find the early temperatures comparatively uncomfortable. A few men, customers, sheepishly joined the congregation, avoiding one another's glances or becoming suddenly intensely interested in pieces of the grimy landscape.

When the Guardians of the Peace returned to the brothel for their quarry, most of the men slunk into the building shadows, quietly fading from the scene. Neither Gill and Rafik, nor Kezdet's officials, bothered to stop them. Though their requirement for paid sexual entertainment humiliated them and would surely wreak havoc with their wives, there was nothing illegal about it. The Guardians sought the Didi herself, to charge her with the attempted murder of Acorna. Each time one of the Guardians emerged from the building with another figure in tow, Gill nudged Rafik. His expectations soared, only to plummet moments later as they left the hapless client or prostitute milling with the others.

The sun crawled higher in the sky, bringing Kezdet's infernal heat. The women ceased hugging themselves, the gooseflesh dissolving into sleek skin over shapely limbs and torsos. Silent women with chattering teeth gave way to huddled groups in conversations that blended into an indecipherable maelstrom of rumbling sound. The Guardians of the Peace escorted one

more figure from the house. "This is the last," one called, the authority in his voice cutting over the din, though only barely.

Gill's elbow flicked out; but, this time, Rafik caught it in his cupped hand. He glared at his friend. "If you do that one more time, I'll break your damned arm."

"Sorry," Gill said in a tiny voice. He had not even realized he had been doing it. He kept his eyes fixed on the newest person to emerge from Badini's brothel, surely the Didi herself.

But the person pinned between the Guardians stood barely taller than their waists, a child with long, soft mahogany hair and wild green eyes. She alternated between kicking, struggling battles and episodes of clinging to a Guardian's leg, sobbing hysterically. Acorna's custodians dashed over to assist.

Gill crouched in front of the child, keeping his face at the level of her own. Tears streaked her cheeks and plastered her bangs to her forehead. Eyes like emeralds sank into deep, hollow sockets. They glanced at him with a flatness that denied life, yet the enthusiasm with which she both battled and embraced the Guardians of the Peace suggested that rape, imprisonment, and possibly torture had not yet fully broken her spirit.

Gill used a soothing tone, perfected among the disenchanted children ferried to Maganos Moon. Even their stalwart belief in, even love for, the woman they called Epona, Sita Ram, or Lukia of the Lights was not enough to prevent the nightmares and terrors from stalking them, especially after dark-time. "It's all right. No one's going to hurt you now."

The girl whimpered, cringing as far away as possible from the enormous redhead, though

that sent her careening against a Guardian's leg. She clamped her lips to bloodless lines, and her hands trembled. Her flailing become less purposeful and more panicky.

The mistrust cut Gill to the quick, but he knew better than to surrender. If he gave up on the girl, she might give up on herself. "We're going to take you back to Acorna."

Nothing about the child changed.

"Epona," Gill tried. Then, "Sita Ram." When the child still did not respond, he added, "She's also called Lukia."

The girl stopped struggling, freezing into a position that would have left her sprawled on the ground if the Guardian of the Peace had not supported her.

"What's your name, child?" Gill tried.

The girl said nothing, only continued to stare. A partially shed tear rolled along her nose, but no new ones formed.

Rafik addressed the Guardian of the Peace. "We'll take her to Mr. Li. She'll be safe there."

The Guardian made a brisk gesture. His companion nodded. "As you wish," the first said. "But be careful. She fights like a tiger." He offered the girl's arm.

Gill accepted the skinny limb carefully, afraid to bruise the delicate flesh. Amid so many full-figured women, she looked boxy and slight. Her silken hair fell straight to her back, and her limbs jutted thinly from a breastless, hipless body wrapped in a white polysilk garment that covered her from neck to knees. Disdain for the men who chose to couple with children rose to a swift crescendo that flared to fiery outrage. Though a man of peace, Gill found a foreign idea flitting joyfully through his mind: for the moment, the thought of slaughtering these perverts found a happy, if temporary, home.

As soon as the Guardians of the Peace released the girl to the custody of Gill and Rafik, she bolted in terror. Gill's sympathetic grip snapped like a twig, and Rafik scarcely fared better. Uncertainty held Gill rooted in place. He knew he did not have the words to stop her, but his nature would not allow him to give chase.

Rafik, however, did not suffer from the same paralyzing scruples. After three running steps, he dove for the hapless child. He managed to catch an ankle, slamming himself and the girl onto the hard edges of shattered cobbles. A cloud of road dust enveloped them, Rafik's voice emerging in a hoarse choke. "Damn it, Gill. Get over here and help me."

Gill sauntered carefully to man and girl as the dust resettled. "Rafik, don't hurt her."

"Hurt her, hell!" Rafik roared. "I'm trying to keep her from hurting herself."

At that moment, the girl whirled on Rafik, clawing at his arms and face.

"Ouch, damn it. Help me." Slitting his eyes against the attack, he kept his one hand on her ankle, grabbing a flailing arm with the other. "She'll die out on the streets. The derelicts in this neighborhood'll do worse than Badini's clients. I'd consider her lucky if you-know-who finds her."

Finally convinced that holding the girl captive would prove in her own best interests, Gill reluctantly assisted his friend. Together, they first pinioned her to the roadway, then hefted her to her feet and led her to the waiting skimmer. Once aboard, she ceased struggling, though quiet tears glimmered on her lashes and trickled in long streams to her chin.

Sighing deeply, Gill rubbed grit from his eyes, only then noticing the irregular checker-

board pattern of scratches that marred Rafik's brown cheeks.

At the first glimpse of Acorna, the girl calmed. Worn out by her ordeal, she barely ate before climbing gratefully into the offered bed and

in a sleep shed or basement. Possibly, her parents had only just sold her into bond labor in the last few weeks or she had become orphaned in that time. Yet, the idea that they had failed a child, any child, narrowed her pupils to vertical slits of grief and anger.

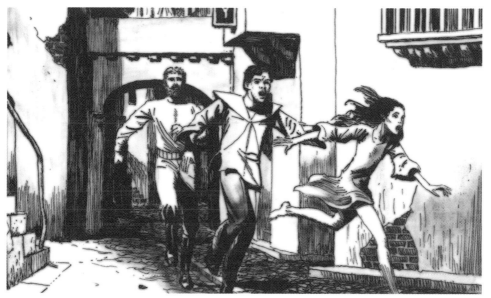

dropping into sleep. Acorna nuzzled away every scratch with her horn, humming lullabies to the rhythm of the fan rotating lazily in the high-ceilinged room. Once she had comforted the girl, she gave her own sorrow free rein. *Somehow,* she thought, *we missed this child when we collected the others.* Guilt suffused her, even knowing that the child may not have come to Kezdet until after their raid or that someone might have hidden her locked

Acorna paced, a display of frustration inadvertently borrowed from Pal Kendoro. Her thick, double-toed feet sank into the carpeting. Hard floors suited her better, yet, she appreciated the muffling of any noise that might wake up her newest charge.

Acorna's mind slid to the five children who had rescued her from Didi Badini's brothel. Their faces filled her mind's eye, perfect in every detail. She recalled Sanga's

cough which she had never healed and the hand Charlas had slid to her privates. Hannoh's words seemed to echo in her brain: "There are others who could use your help, if you can spare it, Lady." *I can spare it*, Acorna told the image in her head. *But I have to find you first.*

Acorna shortened her stride, walking only a few steps before swinging back the opposite direction. Rafik's stern lecture had ended with a forced promise that she would stay off Kezdet's streets unless all five of the men knew her destination and route and at least one accompanied her. Rafik's uncle, Hafiz, had reminded her that Li's potent and exhaustive security would alert them at once, on at least three cameras, if she tried to sneak away without their knowledge.

Acorna might have found Hafiz's warning insulting had her mind not become so fully and obsessively focused on those lost children. True, her original source of information had, apparently, been Didi Badini; and the madam's true purpose for calling Acorna to her shop had been revenge rather than concern for the children. Yet, it had become clear that at least some of what the Didi had written was truth. The children had confirmed the existence of a man indoctrinating them into a life of crime and exploiting them into stealing for his own gain. That would have to end. Acorna had to find a way to tell the children about Maganos Moon Mining, Ltd. They needed to know they had another option, a place to live happily with schools, normal working hours, and jobs that not only gave them a sense of self-worth and accomplishment, but also taught them valuable skills they could continue to use for a lifetime.

But how? Acorna's paced distances grew so short they spiraled into nothingness. She stood in the center of the room, wracked with a sadness that her own vow kept her from remedying. She had no choice but to trust Li's contacts, Pal's computer search, Hafiz's unsavory informational routes, and Gill and Rafik's search of the area where she had met the children and they had discovered her. She glanced toward the figure on the bed. *The child needs me,* she thought. The distraction helped to soothe her frazzled nerves and, at least for the moment, to hold the obsession at bay.

❀   ❀   ❀

At the Manjari mansion, Didi Badini snuggled into a posh recliner that seemed perfectly contoured to her lush curves and solid limbs. Propping her feet on a glass-topped table, she studied Kisla's wan figure at the window. The younger woman's hands clenched the ledge so tightly her fingers blanched. Her skinny torso seemed as rigid as a guard at his post.

"A centi-credit for your thoughts," the Didi said, mostly to break a silence that had become oppressive over the last several minutes.

Kisla's hands winched even more firmly, if such was possible. "I slept on it, and I still want that bitch dead more than anything in the world."

Didi Badini shared Kisla's hatred, but not its intensity. "More than anything?"

"I'd give up my personal spacecraft." Kisla finally pried her fingers loose of the plastic and whirled to face Didi Badini. "I'd give up what's left of my personal fleet. Every ship that misshapen bitch and her reeking brats didn't get in the settlement."

Knowing Kisla loved her top-of-the-line fliers better than any human, Didi Badini nodded thoughtfully. Once, the baron's daughter had harbored dreams of becoming a space navigator and had even gone through nav training. But that would have proven beneath her family's status, so she had flown her toys for no one but herself. These had become her greatest joy, her freedom from the baron's over-bearing parenting. Yet, since her parent's death, she had not gone on to fulfill this fantasy, shackled as much by the desperate need for revenge as she had once been by her father's demands, casual blows, and tight rein over her allowance. He had lent her craft to the saviors of Kezdet's worthless ragamuffins, and Baron Manjari had paid for his crimes against

Kezdet and Acorna (whom he had attempted to murder) not only with money but with several of Kisla's personal ships.

One by one, Didi Badini matched the fingers of her hands into a tent. She leaned over her stiffly-held fingers. "Kisla, if you really mean that, I believe it can be arranged."

Interest kindled in Kisla's cold, blue eyes. She approached the Didi, first hesitantly, then with bold assurance, and took a seat in the opposite chair. "What are you thinking?"

"I'm thinking," Didi Badini said carefully, gaze locked on Kisla's face for the earliest reaction. "Of murder."

Kisla dropped her gaze with a snort of contempt. "We tried that," she reminded.

"Yes." Didi Badini repeated with different emphasis, "We tried that."

"And failed," Kisla reminded.

"And failed," the Didi confirmed.

"She's unkillable."

Didi Badini sat back into the elegant folds of the recliner, tiny bells on her anklets tinkling high-pitched music with the movement. She dropped her hands to the arms of the chair. "You've said that before. You were wrong, then. And you're wrong, now."

Again, Kisla loosed a thick, derisive noise. "If you know how to kill her, why didn't you do it when we had her trapped?"

Didi Badini started an elaborate gesture, but one of her gold bracelets hooked on the fabric of the chair. She worked on surreptitiously freeing it with her opposite fingers, instead. "I didn't know then, but I do now."

Kisla's lids narrowed, sparse lashes striping irises and pupils. Despite that, a glimmer of interest shone through. "What's changed?"

"Research." Didi Badini inclined her head toward the vid screen hovering in an upper corner of the room as she finished untangling her jewelry from the upholstery. "And a lot of directed thought." She placed emphasis on the word "directed," hoping Kisla would take the hint that rage should not be allowed to completely overtake rationality. A dash of hate kept the mind fresh. Too much squelched logic.

Kisla's expression did not change. "Don't tell me. There're vid cubes on how to murder unkillable mutants."

Ignoring the sarcasm, the Didi explained. "There are vid cubes on unicorn legends and myths about ki-lin. You saw her stick that horn thing into a poisoned drink then gulp it down without harm. We both watched her wave that blasted protuberance and turn carbon monoxide back to breathable gases. That perfectly matches the stories that say unicorns can purify water and air."

Tension melted from Kisla, her form seeming almost to flow into a more normal position in the chair. "There're rumors she performs miracles, too. And definitive proof

that she's healed scars, birthmarks, burns, and wounds."

"Indeed." Didi Badini sought some evidence that Kisla, who now possessed nearly as much information as herself, had deduced what had to follow. But, as the baron's daughter simply sat in a dense and deliberate silence, the Didi continued. "She can heal even fatal wounds, can cure cureless diseases, can restore what even our top surgeons cannot." She crowed triumphantly, "But she can't do those things if she's dead!"

Kisla's nose crinkled, and she gave Didi Badini a withering look. "You're talking in circles."

"No."

"You're saying she can't die because she can heal fatal wounds, but she can't heal fatal wounds if she's dead."

"Exactly!" Didi Badini's frustration with Kisla's blind spot increased a thousandfold. The girl was not stupid, only dazzled by anger from understanding this one thing. "To kill her, one simply needs to do so in one blow. Nothing slow or repetitive will work against Acorna. No poison can bring her down. But one perfect shot…"

Kisla surged bolt upright in her chair. A pulse throbbed in her scrawny neck. "You know enough violence to deliver that one perfect shot?"

Didi Badini sighed. "Not me…" She barely refrained from adding "idiot." "An assassin. Hired with your money. Or paid for with your personal space craft, if you so choose."

"You can arrange that?"

"In an instant."

For the first time that day, Kisla managed a broad smile. "Hire the best, Badini. Whatever the cost."

The vast, impenetrable darkness of the aptly named Tunnel to Hell crushed in on Didi Badini, who already felt lightheaded from the chemical-laced air. Only the need to concentrate on the proper jogs and turns, entrusted to memory, kept her from focusing with desperate obsession on the urge to strike a light. More than one curious passerby or medal-seeking Guardian of the Peace had lit the underground conduit that, by ancient rumor, had once served as a means of public transportation. No matter whether its source was energy or heatless, illumination would ignite the deadly blend of gases that the assassin's guild pumped regularly inside. The Didi cringed at the thought of the resultant explosion tearing through the hapless light-bearer, the fireball instantly charring companions' lungs and the smudged and shattered roof stones burying anything that remained.

The blackness swiftly grew oppressive. Didi Badini found herself instinctively, determinedly seeking a shred of light from a pinhole or crack, though she knew she would not find it. Her eyes ached from the futile effort of straining for

shades of gray amidst the pitch. She snapped her lids closed, forcing herself to fixate on the proper route. Craving something reassuring, a tactile landmark if not a visual one, she found her hand drifting toward the wall. A remembered warning echoed through her head: "Touch nothing, or you may discover the contact poison spotting the walls at irregular intervals." She shivered at a tragedy closely averted, jerking back her questing fingers and thrusting them into her pocket.

The ten minute walk to the door felt more like an hour. Then, suddenly, Didi Badini ran out of directions, knowing she stood in front of an unseen polysteel panel and wishing she had not yet arrived. For all its discomfort, blindness felt preferable to the anticipated confrontation. Swallowing hard, she discovered her mouth had gone dry as desert sand, even as her palms developed a light coating of sweat. As delay, she pondered why fear had such odd and opposite

effects on her body. It seemed logical to lick the sweat from her hands to transfer the liquid to a tongue that had become glued to the inside of her right cheek. Irrational images that the slime on her palms actually represented toxins from an unremembered brush against the walls, as well as cultivated class, kept her from doing so. It seemed impossible that her mouth could be so dry when her bladder felt so distressingly full.

Finally, Didi Badini managed to curl and raise a fist. Even then, it hovered in the air several seconds before she gathered the nerve to tap on the door in the complicated sequence her contact had described.

The panel eased open on silent hinges, revealing a small room lit by an opaque, overhead bulb of low wattage. Not even a wisp of light escaped into the hallway. Though remarkably dull, its sudden presence blinded Didi Badini, and she blinked away the colored afterimages striping her retinas.

RE YOU GOING TO COME IN?" A THICK VOICE DRAWLED. "Or just stand there staring stupidly?"

Slowly, Didi Badini's eyes adjusted. A figure dressed in a baggy, black sweatshirt with the hood pulled over his face sat behind an antique desk that appeared to be made of real wood. A closed door interrupted the wall at his back. A hard, plastic chair occupied the center of the room, directly across from the man, with the desk between them.

Didi Badini stepped inside. The man jabbed a button on the arm of his chair, and the door swung shut behind her with a click that tensed every muscle in her body.

"Sit," the man said, his face obscured in shadow. Only his eyes seemed clear, icy gray, and filled with menace.

Didi Badini perched on the edge of a chair that seemed deliberately constructed for discomfort.

"Did you come for business or only to volunteer as a statue at my doorstep?"

This time, Didi Badini had heard enough to recognize the voice. That tiny measure of control induced a courage of which she had, thus far, managed little. She whispered his name.

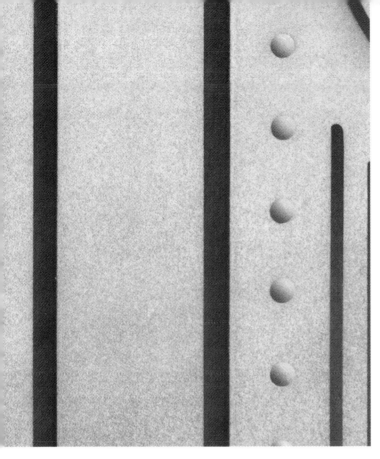

"Janobeck Krinkorolus."

The darkness inside the hood seemed to frown. "Your business?" he reminded in a hiss.

Didi Badini could have pinched her ear off for revealing her knowledge. If an assassin of his competence desired to remain anonymous, it seemed safer to abide by his wishes. "There's someone I need...handled."

"Who?"

The Didi leaned forward. "A woman who goes by the name Acorna."

Janobeck tapped his knuckles together. "The mutant who toppled Kezdet's economy?"

Eagerly, Didi Badini nodded. "The very one."

Janobeck sat back thoughtfully, fists still pressed together.

Didi Badini suspected he could fulfill other contracts on Acorna's head simultaneously and become wealthy with a single murder. Many factory owners and corrupted government officials would rejoice in, and pay for, her death, as well.

The assassin flicked his fingers at the Didi, a brisk gesture of obvious dispatch. "Good day, ma'am. I'm afraid that one is beyond my reach."

"Wait." Didi Badini did not rise, instead clamping the edge of the desk between her fingers. Its smoothness revealed that the construction she had mistaken for wood was actually a thickly pressed plastic, impressively patterned. "She's back on-planet."

The cowled head cocked. "Where?"

"At the Li mansion."

Janobeck slumped back into his chair. "Good day, ma'am. She's definitely beyond my reach."

Didi Badini gathered her legs beneath her, preparing to depart, already cringing from the tongue lashing Kisla Manjari would inflict on her.

Now it was Janobeck's turn to say, "Wait."

Didi Badini looked at him, brows rising slowly with interest.

"If you can lure her to me, I can take care of it."

"Here?"

The head rolled inside the hood's shadows. "Not here." Then, more emphatically, "Absolutely not here."

Hope rising, Didi Badini gripped the arms of her chair. "Where then?"

A short silence followed. Then, Janobeck suggested, "Farsiri's alley. No earlier than dusk." He studied Didi Badini through eyes reflecting cold anger. "You pick the day."

The Didi pursed her lips, suddenly faced with the realization that she might not find a way to entice Acorna anywhere, especially in East Celtalan. She had already played her best card, her knowledge of the Dodger's gang. Yet, the solution followed naturally from the thought. "Three days." She chose randomly, leaving herself enough time to operate and hoping Acorna's interest in rescuing the children kept her on Kezdet that long.

"Three days," Janobeck confirmed. "Dusk?" he guessed.

"Just after," Didi Badini supplied, doubting even her idea would draw Acorna too far beyond darkfall.

Janobeck crossed his legs, drifting toward the desk. "Half million credits. In barter."

"Quarter." Didi Badini haggled Kisla's money with a bored nonchalance she would never have used with her own, even if she had millions of credits to bargain. "Since I have to bring her to you."

Janobeck settled. "Quarter, then, if the goods are solid."

By "solid," Didi Badini knew he meant easily sold for worth. Space craft should qualify. She rose, then realized they had more to discuss. "What are you going to use?"

"Use?" Janobeck's neck craned in question.

"To do the job," Didi Badini supplied.

Janobeck loosed a noise that, though wordless, revealed irritation. "I make it a habit not to discuss my methods with clients."

The Didi did not doubt his claim. "Acorna's different. That horn of hers can fix poisons and cure wounds. Without something swift, accurate, and fatal, you will undoubtedly fail."

The assassin's hand scarcely seemed to move; yet, a moment later, a laser pistol lay on the desk in front of him. "Will this do, Didi?"

Her eyes rolled to the dulled and darkened metal, so unobtrusive it seemed to absorb rather than reflect the sparse light. The nervousness that had assailed her since the contact faded, replaced by a cruel grin. "Perfect," she said.

"Three fatal blasts," Janobeck promised. "And I will not miss." His tone left no room for doubt.

Didi Badini reveled in the perfect excitement that accompanied an infallible plan. The universe itself seemed to align in harmony with her intentions. This time for certain, Acorna would die. "I'm sure you won't," she said, unable to emit anything louder than a whisper. She turned to leave.

"And Didi?"

Badini turned, surprised to find that the pistol had disappeared in that instant. "Yes?"

"Free advice. I don't give it often." Having assured the significance of his next words and her attention, he continued, "Don't go back to your…place of business."

Didi Badini stared. This was not part of the deal.

"Goats." Janobeck used the street term for Kezdet's Guardians of the Peace. "They tossed it. And staked the place out for your return."

Didi Badini growled, her hatred for Acorna trebling in that moment. Only the mutant's powerful companions could have initiated such a thing. "Thanks," she huffed out from between clenched teeth. Opening the door, she disappeared back into the charcoal depths of the Tunnel of Hell.

Through the day and into the night, Rafik and Gill explored the roads and alleyways of East Celtalan, finding a tech-level decades behind the main city and pervading filth that would try the sanity of a mindless housekeeping machine. The human inhabitants matched their ill-kept community: their faces somber, their clothing grimy and patchwork, their bodies sorely in need of a bath. Even after hours of winding though narrow roadways, chasing every tiny sound, Gill found himself incapable of adjusting to the stench of unwashed humans. At least he had managed to stop gagging and even to keep down the robust breakfast Delszaki Li had provided. It contented his stomach until dinner time, when he and Rafik force-swallowed greasy hunks of meat they preferred not to identify, tasteless rubbery cheese, and shriveled fruits with dusky skins and frequent bruises purchased at a grubby little market near the river.

Twilight sent merchants and customers scurrying home, their forms bobbing darkly through the growing evening haze. It also brought a sprinkling of rain. At first, Gill appreciated the change. The light droplets pattering on his scalp brought relief from Kezdet's heat. It also settled the dust kicked up by the mass exodus of East Celtalan's population to the safety of their homes for the night. But, as the last edge of sun tipped over the horizon, the rain quickened and

turned icy. Night breezes buffeted Gill with sharp pinpoints of wet coldness, and the cover of clouds turned the night to a blackness that Maganos and her sister moon rarely punctuated. He saw no stars at all.

Huddled beneath the hood of his overshirt, Rafik cursed softly. "Even the muggers and murderers know better than to drag themselves out in this weather."

Gill pulled on the jacket that had seemed a ridiculous burden through most of the day. "We promised Acorna," he reminded.

"I don't remember promising to freeze myself to death on a fool's errand," Rafik grumbled.

Gill did not bother to dredge up details. Rafik surely recalled them as well as he did. "Well, you did. So stop whining and keep looking."

The two men shuffled along a main street, then turned into an alley umbrellaed by over-hangs. Rafik resumed his lament. "Why can't we be the ones punching consoles and searching data bases? It's not like we don't have any experience."

Gill sighed. The buildings now protected them from the rain but not from the biting wind that stabbed through every gap in their clothing. "Your uncle's got connections you haven't inherited yet. And Li—"

Rafik interrupted, squeegeeing water from the black hanks of hair escaping his hood. "It was a rhetorical question."

"Ahh." Gill glanced at his companion. Cued only by Rafik's sudden stop, he went still as well, centimeters from a waterfall created by a convergence of gutters and a missing roof tile. Startled, he jerked backward, snagging his heel on an abandoned metal can. It clanged aside, revealing a recess in the wall filled with a no-longer-hidden adolescent male.

The boy sprang to his feet and darted for the exit.

"Hey!" Rafik sprinted after him, Gill joining the chase a moment later. "Hey," the swarthy asteroid miner repeated. "Wait! We won't hurt you."

"We just want to talk," Gill tried.

The young man pounded through the alley to the main street, neither losing nor gaining ground. Yet, soon, the home familiarity advantage granted him a few moments to catch hold of a nearby wall. As Rafik and Gill reached him, panting, he scurried to the roof, disappearing into the gloom. His shoes thudded across tile.

"We just want to talk," Gill shouted to the empty darkness, panting mildly between words.

"We work with Epona. We came to help."

Rafik seized his companion's arm. "Forget it. He's long gone."

Gill continued to stare upward several moments, fruitlessly attempting to carve a presence from the hovering clouds as the rain diminished to a fine drizzle.

"Small favors," Rafik muttered at the dwindling droplets, shaking his wet hair. Plastered into clumps, the black locks flew and landed, clinging in new positions on his forehead, cheeks, and neck.

Gill grunted, uncertain he agreed. Once he had become soaked, the new rain did not bother him. It had felt almost warm. Now, the evaporating moisture intensified every breeze into an ice-grained agony. *For Acorna,* he reminded himself as he once had Rafik. *And for the children.* Snuggling deeper into his jacket, he pressed into another narrow thoroughfare. Kezdet's secondary moon struggled through shredding clouds, reflecting enough light to obviate the need for handlights. Churned by the rain, the footing became a treacherous soup of garbage and mud that threatened to claim his shoes.

"This way," Rafik suggested, dragging Gill toward an equally narrow but well-paved corridor wedged between endless rows of identical, boxy homes. That brought them back to a dry main roadway that gave off the faint, sour odor of rain

repellent. "Ahh," Rafik said, head shifting and eyes never still. "Slum technology." Skimmers had long ago ended the need for skid-free highways, except as walkways; and newer surfacing materials made the pathways of the rest of the city safe without the need for outdated chemicals.

Too focused on his discomfort, Gill did not bother with a reply. Mist wove across his face and hands, even as his clothes no longer felt heavily sodden. The two men fell into an empty silence, punctuated by the occasional slam of a door, the mechanical clicks of some appliance set into motion or the low, steady buzz of an idling skimmer. As they slid back into an alley, glazed by the damp moonlight that managed to struggle through wisps of clouds, an argument from a nearby cottage joined the other sounds of East Celtalan, a man and a woman shouting about credits and the relative merits of food versus entertainment.

Rafik gestured at another nameless alley, and Gill swiveled toward it, nodding. Shielded by overhanging eaves, it admitted only scanty dribbles of moonlight. Rafik switched on his handlight, the beam playing over packed earth that was sandy enough to absorb the rain. At the farthest edge of the bright circle, something moved.

Rafik jerked up his light in time to catch several small, running figures in the beam. Their feet made little sound on the semi-solid roadway,

and gouts of sand flew in awkward arcs, kicked up in their wake. "Wait!" he shouted. "We just want to talk." He darted after the retreating forms as they disappeared from the extent of his light. Gill chased after his companion. The handlight beam bobbed with his every movement, occasionally catching a heel or arm in its light. The alleyway came to an abrupt end, branching into a five-way intersection of pathways of varying widths. Rafik skidded to a stop, scanning each direction with his light.

A sound from the right hand wall sent Gill spinning, drawing and clicking on his own handlight. Soft, white glare materialized on the wall, revealing a young girl scrambling through a shattered, third story window. "Please," Gill called gently to her. "We just want information." He listened for movement, his heart pounding. As long as she remained hidden in place instead of running, she might hear him. "We're friends of Epona."

"Sita Ram," Rafik tried, his light cutting patterns across each of the pathways.

"We're looking for a man called the Dodger."

No answer followed. Then, small footsteps drummed across a hardwood floor overhead, retreating.

"Damn," Gill said, the curse soft after his previous shouting, yet oddly more effective for the contrast.

"This is pointless." Turning, Rafik played his light over the window through which the girl had disappeared. "They're not going to listen without Acorna."

Gill knew his partner spoke truth, but he refused to give up, yet. "Just through the night." He turned Rafik a hard look. "We need to give it that long."

Rafik chewed his lower lip, his stance revealing that he believed only lost sleep would result. As Gill braced for an argument, he said, "Fine." Rafik raked wet strands of hair from his cheeks. "I'm not convinced shouting our intentions at scared kids gains us anything, but..." He left the rest of the sentence unspoken, switching to another. "We leave at first sunlight."

"First sunlight," Gill agreed, thinking it best not to mention a new concern that Rafik's words had raised. If this secretive Dodger heard them calling his name all over East Celtalan, he might come or send someone to silence them, not necessarily a bad thing. At least that meant they would find him. *Hopefully, a man used to working with injured children will talk before turning to anything more drastic and deadly.*

Rafik chose a walkway at random, and Gill trotted after his companion. A chill jerked through him, unrelated to the cold. The hairs on the nape of his neck rose. Everywhere now, he saw twitching shadows, heard sounds where none existed. *Stop it*, he told himself. *Paranoia*

won't help. Glancing behind more often then ahead, he crashed into Rafik hard enough to send his slighter partner staggering several steps forward. Rafik whirled on him with a warning glare, then gestured toward the approaching dead-end with a jerk of his head.

Rubbing the bruise Rafik's elbow had gouged into his chest, Gill looked in the indicated direction. A man slouched against the wall near a door surrounded by peeling pillars striped with dirt. Hair dark with filth hung in greasy clumps, its original color unguessable. Tattered clothing two sizes too small stretched over flabby limbs and left a paunch exposed. Rain dribbled, parting trails through his hairy belly. Chokingly thick, the stench of rancid flesh drifted to Gill's nose, and his stomach lurched.

"Hello," Rafik said.

The stranger belched. "Oh-lay-ho!" he slurred out. "OH-LAY-HO!" He made a clumsy, exaggerated gesture of rejection. The movement sent waves of fetid odor wafting toward them.

Rafik looked at Gill, who shrugged. It sounded like no language he had ever heard.

"Sir?" Gill tried, tasting bile and fighting not to gag.

Lids speckled with tiny yellow growths crinkled, adding wrinkles to an already ravaged face. His eyes seemed to disappear into the flesh. "What do you want?" Then, much louder. "What do you want?!"

"Too many happy-sticks," Rafik guessed.

Gill shook his head. Happy-sticks had become the primary means of entertainment specifically because they were not addictive or dangerous, providing a high without risk. "More likely a chronic psychological ailment. Or long-term use of an archaic pleasure."

"Thank you for your brilliant diagnosis, Dr. Gilloglie," Rafik said with mock solemnity.

No longer slumping, the man stood stiffly in the street, gaze locked on Gill and Rafik. "What do you want?" he demanded again.

"Let's go," Rafik said.

"Wait." Gill refused to dismiss a possible source of information out of hand, no matter how unlikely. *At least, we've got him talking sense, now.* "We want only information. What do you know?"

"I know lots of things." The man continued to speak in an uncomfortably loud voice, his breath smelling like something dead left to rot in the sun. He rolled his eyes in a wild circle. "And nothing."

"Gill...," Rafik started.

Gill waved his companion silent, addressing the stranger again. "Do you know of a man called the Dodger?"

The cracked lips came together, the lower brown with old blood. A wispy beard followed the chin, clotted with dirt, juices and crumbs.

When no words emerged after several moments, Gill began again, louder. "Do you know—?"

"No!" the man cried out suddenly, the word sharp and echoing.

Involuntarily, Gill back-stepped. Rafik grumbled something about "ludicrous" and "wasted time."

Gill adamantly refused to leave the first person who had not run from them without first trying every way to extract information. "Would a five-credit chit help you remember?"

"Gill…," Rafik said again, this time warningly. He had already expressed his disdain for a planet that still dealt, even in a small way, with untraceable currency. The attitude seemed odd coming from one who would inherit an empire built almost exclusively on such loopholes in the credit system.

Frowning, Gill gave his head a single shake. They had brought the chits specifically for this purpose, to jog memories.

The grubby man's eyes followed Gill's hand as it dipped into his pocket and emerged with the dark disk balanced on his palm. "Might help," he croaked.

Gill turned Rafik a smug grin. Their first breakthrough had come with persistence, as he had repeatedly stated it would. He stepped toward the stranger, realizing as he did that exchanging the chit might result in a touch by a malodorous crazy man who could turn unpredictably violent. Acid roiled in his nearly empty stomach. Pinching the chit by an edge, he held it out to the grungy stranger.

The man snatched the coin, every crease in his hand etched with a dark line of dirt. The hand disappeared into his pants momentarily, then snaked back into sight, without the chit.

As Gill stepped back, Rafik relaxed visibly. "So," Gill said, "Do you know of the Dodger, now?"

The stranger rubbed his belly, smearing sludge across the hairy, white skin. "Nope." He looked up. "Sorry. Nope. Never heard of him."

"Never?" Gill repeated, incredulous.

"Never." The man smiled, exposing several gaps between yellowed teeth.

"But you took my credits."

The man shrugged, his sleeves drawing even further up his forearms, revealing knobby elbows. Another recking belch escaped him. "Wouldn't you do the same?"

Gill hoped he would never find himself in the position to know. "Can you tell us anything?

Perhaps you've seen a group of children working together?"

"There's gangs around here." He scratched his beard, freeing unidentifiable flakes and a single madigadi seed. "Ain't never been asked to join 'em." A coarse laugh erupted from him, little different from the belch, except it became a sustained sound. He crumpled to a sitting position on the ground, suddenly rigid. "Oh-lay-ho," he said, as before, arms flapping through the air. "OH-LAY-HO!" Baring his teeth in an animal snarl, he glared at the two men with whom he had chatted a moment before.

"Do you still—" Gill led off the question, interrupted by the stranger's lunge toward them.

Gill and Rafik scrambled several paces down the alley, the attack breaking off as abruptly as it occurred. Apparently satisfied by the retreat, the man shook his head, ropes of hair splattering filth, and settled back into his slouched position.

"Come on." Rafik seized Gill's arm, his tone surprisingly gentle for one who had accurately assessed a situation contradicted by a no-longer gloating companion. "Let's keep looking."

"I'm sorry," Gill felt obligated to say as they selected another corridor. "I was hoping—"

Rafik cut him off. "I know. I was hoping, too." He led the way through dingy streets that began to look alike. "Sometimes the best knowledge does come from the least likely places."

People act and speak freely in front of those they believe too demented to comprehend them."

This time, it was Gill's turn to grouse. "He understood credits well enough."

"Maybe." Rafik did not even seem sure of that. "He could have talked more out of us. He could have made us believe he knew something, without actually promising anything, then eased another fifteen credits from us." He shrugged, detailing other possibilities. "Or more. We probably would have kept feeding him chits so long as he made up plausible enough lies."

Gill studied his long-time partner. "You're scaring me, Rafik."

"How so?"

"You're getting as twisty as your uncle."

An odd grin crept across Rafik's swarthy features, half-hidden in the gloom. He borrowed an ancient expression, "You said that like it's a bad thing."

Conversation died as the two men continued through East Celtalan's poorly maintained walkways, sandwiched between sagging hovels, crumbling businesses and warehouses. Time dried their water-logged clothing, and the winds warmed as midnight dragged toward daytime. The clouds frayed into lacy patterns, opening the sky, then gradually balled into haphazard, white designs. Pink touched the horizon.

Rafik poked a finger toward the approaching sunrise. "Time."

"Time," Gill agreed, uncertain whether the weariness that turned his every step into a shuffle was born of a lost night of sleep or disappointment. He waited for Rafik to choose the direction. In the course of meandering through what seemed like thousands of throughways, he had become hopelessly confused. He would never admit such a thing, of course. After negotiating space for years, allowing himself to get lost on-planet would make him look like the world's biggest fool.

Rafik neither suffered from Gill's affliction, nor seemed to notice his partner's uneasiness. Eager to return, he trotted through the maze of alleyways, familiar landmarks sparking Gill's memory as well. They entered a dark, tunnel-like threadway that Gill recalled ended in a tight sequence of buildings. Once they squeezed through the winding pathway beyond, a well-lit and wide-open street would bring them to the skimmer and its waiting driver.

Gill and Rafik had taken only a few steps into the mostly enclosed alley, when a shadow blotted out enough of the funneling light to send both miners spinning toward it. A man stood in the opening. Darkness stole details, but his stance suggested youth. A glimmer of advancing sunlight revealed a line of gold in hair that the gloom would otherwise have rendered dark.

For several moments, no one spoke. Then, the stranger broke the silence. "You the ones looking for the Dodger?"

"Yes," Gill said brightly, a sudden rush of expectation disallowing thought before speech.

The man raised a palm, then beckoned the two deliberately closer.

Rafik and Gill complied. As they drew nearer, the other's features became clearer. A steep forehead gave way to broad cheeks and a prominent nose. By Gill's reckoning, he was in his older teens to early twenties, now definitely blond. His hazel eyes held a dangerous gleam, and the stiff set of his features enhanced the image.

"You boys got chits?"

The shock of an adolescent calling him and Rafik "boy" kept Gill quiet long enough for Rafik to take over the negotiations. "Why do you want to know?"

The stranger glided another pace toward them, now blocking the entrance completely. "You'll need unencumbered credits to see the Dodger." His tone grew impatient. "You got some or not?"

"Yes," Rafik said, gaze fastened on the newcomer and mouth naturally spitting back the stranger's affected dialect. "We got some."

Not many. Just enough to bribe street kids. Gill did not speak aloud. It only made sense to allow the heir to the Harakamian empire to handle shady dealings.

"Let's see them," the young man demanded.

Obligingly, Rafik drew three one-credit chits from his pocket and displayed them in his palm.

"Drop them on the ground." The stranger whipped a stunner from his pocket and pointed it at a spot halfway between Gill and Rafik. "All of them. Now!"

Gill tensed at the ferocity of the final word, eyes locked on the stunner, trying to read the setting through the shadows. Knowing whether the youth planned to kill them or only render them unconscious might help determine their next course of action. But Gill's vision lapsed into a painful blur of dryness, and his chest seemed to squeeze shut.

Rafik dumped the three chits in the mud.

The man shook the stunner. "I said all of them. And any other valuables you might be wearing or carrying."

Gill lost track of his companion, desperate to comply, yet abruptly frozen in place. *Nothing I own is worth losing my life.* Yet, his limbs refused to obey, capable only of trembling. Panic raced down on him. *I'm going to die because I'm too scared of dying to move.* Even through the fog scrambling his thoughts, the irony reached him.

"Do it." The stranger's voice filled with threat.

Without a word, Rafik charged the youngster.

"No!" Gill screamed. Paralysis disappeared in an instant. He sprang for his friend, missed, and slammed into the cobbles. A bolt of white light flashed through his head, and pain hammered his right cheekbone. Grit billowed into his eyes, hot pinpoints of agony. Blinking wildly, he scrambled to a crouch. Rafik and the stranger rolled across stone, enveloped in a cloud of dust. Arms flailed. Their bodies writhed, avoiding bone-jarring impacts even as each attempted to score punches on the other. The stunner clicked against cobble. Gill lurched toward it as a wild kick sent it skittering far into the gloom. He watched it carom from a wall, casing shattering, then the largest piece of the remains glided through a gutter hole.

Returning his attention to the fight, Gill hovered, awaiting an opening. As the two drew back for momentum simultaneously, they momentarily separated. Gill rushed in like an enraged bull. The stranger jerked backward, took one look at the massive figure flying toward him, then turned tail and sprinted into East Celtalan's erratic infrastructure. Gill lumbered in pursuit.

Rafik limped after his companion. "Let him go."

Obediently, Gill stopped, watching the would-be mugger's lithe form disappear. Now the sky held a veritable rainbow of colors, the pink giving way to shades of coral and yellow, followed by bands of green and a brilliant sapphire that encompassed the remaining sky. The first edge of Kezdet's sun crowned the horizon.

Fear dispersed before a growing sense of outrage. Gill whirled toward Rafik. "You stupid, reckless moron! What the hell were you thinking?" He did not await an answer. "Was it really worth risking our lives for twenty credits of chits, a ring and a lousy embroidered handkerchief?" Only then, he noticed the rip in Rafik's left pant leg, revealing the angry red blotches that would shortly become bruises. His nose dribbled blood, and his right eyelid had swollen nearly shut.

Rafik studied his companion's face through slitted eyes, though only one deliberately so. "I thought I was the one who took all the blows." He reached for Gill's cheek. "What happened to you?"

Gill jerked away, only then suffering the throbbing head and cheek ache from his fall. "I had a run-in with the ground trying to stop you from getting us both killed." He rubbed at the wound, then wished he had not. Pain stabbed through his cheek. The right side of his face felt twice its normal size. "And you still haven't explained yourself."

Rafik plucked the three credit chits from the mud, then motioned Gill to continue walking. Moving seemed like a reasonable strategy, since the mugger could return with others and finish what he started. "We weren't in any danger."

Gill snapped his head toward his long-time partner. "How do you figure that?"

Rafik stumbled through the alley, pausing at the end to negotiate the sharp, narrow switchway that would take them to the main road. "I recognized the stunner. It's the type the Guardians of the Peace use."

Trailing Rafik through the narrow passage, Gill could not reconcile Rafik's claim to his explanation. "So. A Guardian's stunner was what killed your cousin, Tapha. Or don't you remember?"

"I remember." Rafik emerged onto the street. Lights burned in the windows of several houses. The colors had already faded from the sky, leaving only the low ball of Kezdet's sun. The Guardians of the Peace had shot Hafiz's son and displaced heir, Tapha, when he entered the docks with a bomb intended to destroy the asteroid miners and their ship. "My point is the Guardians' stunners are keyed to their fingerprints. This one, obviously stolen, wouldn't function because this guy's fingerprints wouldn't match the guardian he took it from."

As the skimmer hove into view, Gill loosed a sigh of relief. Only now he recalled Pal telling them about the fingerprint matching. In the alleyway, he had not had the presence of mind to try to recognize the stunner's make, let alone put together such details. "Very clever."

"Thank you."

They fast-walked to the skimmer. Only as

they clambered in behind the pilot did the flaw in Rafik's reasoning occur to Gill. "You know, he could have bypassed or changed the fingerprint code."

"Not likely he could afford it, even if he could find someone to do it." Rafik shook his head. "Besides, alteration overloads the power cell. Pal says it's not a pretty sight."

Other options came to Gill. "He could have been a Guardian who quit. Or got fired."

A lengthy pause followed.

Gill looked directly at Rafik, who stared out the window at the disappearing eastside. "Could have been," Rafik said finally, before lapsing into a silence that he would not break until the skimmer drew up to Delszaki Li's compound.

Gill sat back, face aching, glad for the skimmer's closed warmth. He doubted Rafik would ever tell him whether he had considered such minutiae before jumping the mugger in East Celtalan's alley. But now he knew the value of his life to Rafik. *Twenty credits. Twenty stinking credits.*

For reasons Gill would never understand, the whole thing suddenly seemed uproariously funny. His laughter became infectious. By the time they touched down, all three of them were howling.

❊   ❊   ❊

Kisla Manjari's sleeping chambers contained a massive bed draped in zebra-patterned Theloi silk. Each piece matched perfectly, from the sturdy canopy to the velvoit comforter and sheets that stretched, without lumps, over the mattress and pillow mounds. Framed matte vids of myriad space craft covered the walls, ranging from promethean war ships to single-seater skiffs. Kisla sat at a sleek desk, its classic, machine-cut designs rescued from plainness by blown glass swans and waterfalls worked into the motif. An oval mirror rose from the center, perfectly back-lit, now reflecting the face of a child-like stranger.

"That's me?" Kisla asked incredulously. Seated at the desk, she extended her neck until her face nearly touched the surface.

Amused by Kisla's reaction, Didi Badini snapped her make-up case closed. "No, it's Casely. A fourteen-year-old who escaped my 'bonk shop' when the Guardians of the Peace raided it." The words brought a hot flush of anger to her cheeks. She wondered how long she would have to run the brothel through an intermediary, risking her safety and her business every time Runeil made contact. Bribes would help cool the hunt, but she could not compete with Li's vast fortune. Her other "assets," her working women, might not prove enough unless she could discover more of the specialized commodities: children, women who tolerated or even enjoyed violence, and young men down on their luck.

Didi Badini looked at her partner,

swallowing a mouthful of saliva. She had worked with women like Kisla before, stunted and scrawny from an anorexia they embraced as the only controllable portion of their lives. Her late father had ruled his family with the same inflexible severity as his shipping conglomerate and left Kisla with little influence over anything more than what she put into her body. The right hair style or wig, expression training and carefully applied cosmetics easily transformed these girl-figured women into children through their middle age. Then the battle against coarsening features and wrinkling skin turned the facade into a challenge, eventually lost. Didi rarely worried about a gain of self-respect, and consequently of weight, interfering with the process. Dignity and pride disappeared in her service, immediately squelched whenever it stirred.

Kisla's exquisitely preadolescent figure, stick-straight and lacking breasts or stomach, could fill the need left after Acorna and her lackey's raided the brothels. Didi Badini shook the thought away. The spoiled and arrogant baroness would never agree to such a thing.

Kisla interrupted a train of thought she would never have tolerated. "All right, I let you do it." She spun her chair, looking up to Didi Badini no longer standing behind her. "Now, explain."

Didi Badini pulled up the only other chair in the room, a hard, green frame inset with patterned cushions. Sitting, she detailed her idea. "The assassin will wait in a set position. It's our job to bring the deformed mutant to him."

Kisla attempted to guess, "And you think she'll follow me because I look like a child?" Her eyes seemed to penetrate Badini's skull. "Lots of things could go wrong. Not the least of which is that she and her friends will probably recognize me. Even if she dies, I'll be implicated in the crime."

Idiot. Didi Badini shook her head. "That's not it at all." She ran her fingers over the smooth arms of the chair. "At least, hear the plan before you start looking for problems."

Kisla settled back into her seat, but her expression remained skeptical.

Good. If she's looking for holes, she might see something I missed. Didi Badini continued, "Apparently, we piqued her interest. A couple of her accomplices ran around East Celtalan last night asking for the Dodger."

"Fools." Kisla snorted. "They're not going to find him. Couldn't they figure out that's why they call him the Dodger and not, say, the Stupid Deadman?"

"And," the Didi proceeded, talking over her co-conspirator, "there's been a sudden rash of electronic inquiries about the Dodger and his methods. Discrete, to be sure, but all originating from the Li mansion."

Again, Kisla attempted to second guess the

Didi's plan. "You want me to pretend to be one of the Dodger's brats and lure Acorna to the right place?" A frown deeply scored her features, stealing the manufactured youth. "There's still the recognition problem."

"Don't do that," Didi Badini warned, mimicking Kisla's scowl. "Ruins your disguise."

Kisla rolled her eyes. "It's not like I need to pose for you."

"But you leave telltale creases in the paint."

Kisla muttered something negative but nevertheless schooled her features as Didi Badini had taught.

The Didi stole the lapse to reclaim the conversation. "You were about a quarter right this time." She drummed her fingers on the arm rests. "The two of us can't possibly simulate the Dodger's operation well enough to fool Acorna, especially while she's with her companions. Not only is Li a shrewd man, he also has the experience she lacks and that sometimes makes her gullible enough to fall for things like our message."

"Stop that," Kisla growled, gazing at Badini's hands.

Caught in a nervous habit, Didi Badini stilled her fingers. "The only one who could bring Acorna to the indicated spot alone is the Dodger himself."

Kisla stared, struggling against natural

expressions for the good of her disguise. "You have a way to find him?" She switched to the more significant problem. "He'd do that for you?"

"No." Didi Badini answered both questions simultaneously. "I'm the enemy, remember? One of the people he rescues children from. His work gang stole Acorna from us."

Kisla drew breath, head weaving side to side. "I don't understand."

Discovering herself about to lapse back into tapping, Didi Badini laced her fingers beneath her chin. "If I can get to him, I can convince him she's as much a danger to him as to us. The trick…" She leaned toward Kisla. "…and the place you come in, is finding him."

A glow of understanding swept Kisla's eyes. "I'm a fourteen-year-old girl who escaped your 'bonk shop' during the raid of the Guardians of the Peace."

"You're stuck on the streets with nowhere to go and no means of support, terrified of starving or falling prey to gangs or worse. And you happen to know some information the Dodger may find interesting—a plan in which he might like to play a role, even if it means a temporary truce with one he normally considers an enemy."

Kisla's pursed lips suggested she found the idea worthy of consideration.

Didi Badini sat back, hands still folded together, awaiting Kisla's doubts and objections.

The baroness did not disappoint, "What if the children who rescued the mutant saw us working together and recognize me?"

Anticipating the question, Didi Badini smiled. "They didn't notice you. If they had, you would already have suffered the pleasure of a visit from Kezdet's Guardians of the Peace, as I did." She awaited more challenges.

Kisla folded her arms over her chest, head cocked in consideration. "It could work," she finally said.

"It will work," Didi Badini asserted, keeping the rest to herself. *It has to.*

Kisla's next question changed the course of the conversation, turning her from interrogator to partner. "You'll help me with my story?"

"Of course, Kisla," Didi Badini said with a smile. "Of course."

"That's Casely," the younger woman corrected.

The crescent of Maganos moon shed scant light over East Celtalan square, turning the lock-covered stands into brooding shadows. Though in its third quarter, the secondary moon added little to Didi Badini's vision. She walked through the north entrance of the empty square, trying to keep her movements graceful and sure but not overconfident. The wary prickle of unseen eyes had tensed her muscles into knots as she traversed the last several walkways to the market, and she hoped the spies belonged to the Dodger and not the Guardians of the Peace. The feeling

had intensified the nearer she drew to the meeting place, becoming reassuring for its familiarity and the increasing certainty of its source.

Didi Badini paused just inside, glancing cautiously in all directions. She wore a Neredian retro-satin that emphasized her full-figured contours while minimizing her belly and hiding her dense thighs. Gold chains and jewel-toned silk scarves added radiant highlights at all the right places. She could not guess the Dodger's intentions or tastes, but dressing attractively for the man seemed only prudent. Where her verbal skills failed, her physical charms might save the negotiation.

The Didi's delay brought a small figure creeping through the rafters of a vegetable stand. The child dropped to the ground near her feet.

Startled by his sudden appearance, Didi Badini back-stepped with a gasp that emerged too quickly to suppress. She studied the boy in the meager light of Kezdet's moon and stars. Dressed in tight-fitting black, he all but faded into the gloom even after his dramatic appearance revealed his precise location. Curled locks the color of night dangled into sapphire eyes, and a prominent chin masculinized otherwise child-soft features. The Didi sucked in another sharp mouthful of air. If this vision had not worked in a brothel, he should have. She would have paid handsomely for a youth of his potential.

"This way," he said, his tone glacial.

Whether his attitude stemmed from an attempt to remain professional, she did not care. She could not help staring.

Didi Badini nodded as the boy turned his back and skittered forward, rewarding her with the scenery of his narrow waist and compact rear end. She noted that he frequently turned his head sideways, watching her and adjusted his pace to remain always beyond her reach. He led her along several pathways trampled by the frequent passage of feet through the market, then abruptly disappeared.

The Didi stopped, seeking the boy through the darkness and nearly missing a young girl who seemed to rise from the ground itself. She made a strange contrast to Badini's previous guide, younger, tiny to the point of delicacy, yet with features disappointingly plain. Squinty eyes hid the color of her irises. An enormous hooked nose jutted from her otherwise dollish face, and her ears stuck out like funnels. This one did not speak, only threaded toward the center of the stalls. Quietly, Didi Badini followed.

Soon, that guide too vanished, leaving the Didi alone amid skeletal, plastic stands fleshed by billowing tarps protecting locked-down covers. The wind carried rain pooled from the previous night, and she worried for the effect of those cold driblets on her perfectly layered cosmetics and powders. The sensation of being watched remained, goading

her not to scratch or to rearrange her clothing. Naturally, the effect of worrying about those things made the the urge to do them nearly irresistible.

A lull twice as long as that between her previous guides ensued. Just as she began to wonder why she had bothered to come at all, a mellow, male voice broke the stillness. "You wished to see me?" He added a single word in a tone dripping distaste, "Didi." The word literally translated into "big sister," but had replaced "madam" in Kezdet's vernacular.

Didi Badini stiffened, ejecting breath through her teeth in a hiss. She looked toward the voice, and gradually discerned an adult male shape from the background. Clearly, he had waited there since before her arrival, dressed in shades of dark gray and silver that virtually disappeared against the shadows. A broad-brimmed hat fully hid his hair and eclipsed his eyes into murky obscurity. A nondescript nose overhung generous lips. Though his pose was nonchalant, casually slouched against a utility pole, a wariness in his manner made it clear he could react in an instant. Realizing she had not addressed his question, she scrambled for a response. "So you are—" she started.

He did not let her finish. "Yes. State your business."

It amazed the Didi how he could convey so much with just his voice. Now she

detected impatient warning. If she did not swiftly snag his interest, she would lose this hard-won meeting and never gain another chance. She realized she needed to leap directly to the point. "There's a woman," she blurted, "with designs on your operation and your children."

The Dodger made a noise of disgust. "That describes even you, Didi." He gave the final word the same ghoulish emphasis as before. At least he was still listening.

Didi Badini gathered her failing morale. "But this one has the Li/Harakamian Consortium behind it, the monies of both empires, and a creature the children of Kezdet worship as a goddess."

The Dodger appeared to stiffen, the movement so slight Didi Badini wondered if she had seen it at all. A high-pitched whistle emanated from him, then three more notes in a musical pattern.

The Didi waited, eyes narrowing in question. Slight sounds followed the nonverbal command, the thuds of feet landing, unidentifiable scrapes and the rustle of fabric. Clearly, the Dodger had signaled his troops that he needed privacy.

A lengthy silence filled the empty market before the Dodger spoke again. Then, he continued as if no time had passed. "Acorna has returned."

"Yes," Didi Badini confirmed. "And she has her eyes on your gang."

"How did she find out?"

"I don't know," the Didi lied. "But she did. And she's put every effort for the last several days into tracking you." The Dodger's apparent ignorance surprised her. "Did you not know about those two guardians of hers who went crashing about last night looking for you?"

"I knew," the Dodger said, either from the need to look in control or from actual awareness. Didi Badini suspected the latter. Surely his vast network of children had seen them and would have informed him. More likely, he had just learned their source and their connection to Acorna.

Didi Badini tightened the noose. "And computers are tapping every legitimate and illegal source for information about you."

A sound issued from the Dodger that Didi Badini did not at first recognize. Eventually, it occurred to her that he was grinding his teeth. "Why me?"

Isn't it obvious? Didi Badini held her tongue. She could not afford to antagonize him, especially when she had him so nearly won to her side. "Because they've stolen most of Kezdet's bonded labor for use on their own moon mining project. They have most of the children who were bonded or sold to places like my own, to the factories, and to the on-planet mines. But like any user of children, they want every single one they can shackle into service. Currently, you have the largest remaining collection." She opened her hands in a gesture to indicate the Dodger should be able to assume the rest on his own.

The Dodger's lips clamped shut. Clearly, he mulled her words and the seriousness of her accusations. "We've hardly been old friends, Didi." This time, his tone contained little of his previous spite. "Why are you telling me this?"

"Because." The Didi tried to keep her expression as stony as his. This time, at least, her intentions were exactly as stated. "We have a common enemy, now. I've laid a trap for her, and I need your help to spring it." She studied him, anticipating a rejection out of hand.

"Explain," the Dodger said evenly.

Didi Badini lowered her voice to a whisper. Though the Dodger surely used his troops to alert him to the presence of strangers or Guardians of the Peace, she felt safer not needing to rely on them, especially after his whistle had removed the closest ones. "Tomorrow night, there'll be an assassin waiting for her in Farsiri's alley. All we need to do is lead her past that position sometime after dusk, and he'll handle the rest."

The Dodger's eyes flickered in the shadows beneath his hat brim. "Done," he said.

Didi Badini smiled, lowering her lids in a coy gesture of partnership.

When she opened them again, the Dodger was gone.

HE POUNDING OF A FIST ON HIS BEDROOM DOOR AWAKENED Pal Kendoro in a heart-hammering instant. Attempting a graceful leap from his bed, he got tangled in his blanket. His first step sprawled him to the floor, all thoughts of refinement fleeing his sleep-dulled mind. Disentangling his legs, he grabbed his robe from the bedside chair, tossed it over his undergarment and shouted, "Come in," before bothering to tie it. The realization that it could be Acorna or a female servant quickened his fingers. He finished the knot as the door wrenched open and Albanoric Telkorum, a senior lieutenant from Li's security division, stepped inside. "Trouble, Pal."

Weariness fled, worry sharpening Pal's wits. "What's happened?"

"I'll explain as we go." Albanoric's over-large head jerked toward the hallway, hair the color and texture of straw scarcely budged by the movement. He stepped aside so that his stocky frame no longer blocked the entire doorway, and Pal slipped through the opening and into the corridor. Albanoric drew up beside Pal. Together, they trotted toward the security monitoring chamber, Albanoric fulfilling his promise along the way. "First perimeter security was breached in eight different places within a minute."

Pal put the details together swiftly. *Eight groups or individuals. Have to be working together.* A chill screwed through him. An invasion.

As Pal and Albanoric neared the monitoring chamber, the shrill of the outer laser alarms filled the corridor. They joined the men and women around various monitors, just as a second band of alarms screamed a duet with the first. Yellow lights blinked on the panel overhead.

"Damn!" A tall, whale-boned woman with graying brown hair pounded on her console. "They've broken the inner lasers, too. In two places."

"Two more here," a nasal voice called from the center of the room.

A young woman in the far corner raised a hand. "I've got three."

"Last one's my area."

Pal did not bother to identify the last speaker. Nudging aside Assistant Chief Shintaris, a club-faced giant with lanky, red hair, he took the other's place in front of a vid screen. His fingers flew across the keys. The screen blanked, then reappeared with confirmation of his prints. The few seconds that interchange cost him dragged like an eternity. He entered his security code to validate the system's findings, then punched up the perimeter cameras, zeroing in on the breaches' lock and feed images. Sixteen squares formed interconnected pictures of the familiar twenty foot walls topped by decorative shrubbery that hid thin beams as fine as wires. Three areas flashed, one external, another amid the bushes and the third on the inner aspect of the stone, indicating disruptions somewhere along each of the security circuits. Then black holes replaced portions of the feed.

Pal glowered. "Bring up number eight."

Albanoric and Shintaris looked over his shoulder.

"Eight's down," the large-framed woman announced. "Along with two, five, eleven and sixteen. Not even a glimpse of who did it."

"Damn!" Pal echoed her previous curse. "What's going on, now?"

An ear-splitting klaxon shattered the lower level warnings that had become familiar.

"Main gate!" someone shouted.

Shintaris waded into the security personnel, many of whom had leapt to their feet, eyes glued to various vid screens. "Fraggit! We know there's a problem. Silence those damn alarms!"

Keys and buttons clicked in sequence, then the noise cut off raggedly, leaving a silence every bit as ominous.

"Cue the video," Pal said. "Number one."

Shintaris added. "And bring up the map grid. Look for patterns."

"Here!" a young man called to Pal, who left his chair for the images backed up on camera one. A clear field gave way to gradual darkness, like a cloud enwrapping the sun. Pal caught a glimpse of a dark hand that quickly skittered beyond the lens. Then came several moments of blank screen while Pal tapped his foot impatiently. The camera itself still functioned, recording nothing. Suddenly, it cleared, leaving an image of the familiar diamond-iron gate securely bolted, its detection beams, set to identify every known weapon and poison, still intact. Beside it, someone had dug out the hidden control panel, and it hung suspended by laser-wires. A modified crowbar lay on the ground.

I don't believe it. In the history of Li's financial and industrial empire, no one had managed a single trespass. Eight at once seemed patently impossible. *This is a dream. This is all a bad dream.* Pal glanced at the map grid, at the eight equidistant, red-flashing splotches on the perimeter where the patently impossible had occurred.

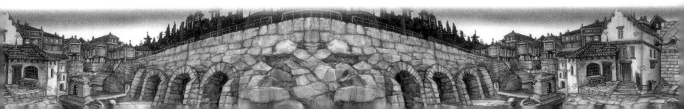

Another deafening alarm blared.

"What this time!" Shintaris hollered. Despite the volume, his voice was barely loud enough to be heard.

Someone killed the newest alarm. A shaky voice informed them, "Th-the weapons panel is dead."

"Dead!" Shintaris dashed to the speaker's side, driven to talk only in exclamation points.

A petite blonde tugged at Pal's sleeve. "Look, sir."

Pal turned his attention back to camera one where four figures worked in tandem, one poking at the controls, another hovering, and the last two jimmying the "unpickable" lock with a tool unlike anything Pal had ever seen. "Zoom in," Pal said.

The input dragged the four to the foreground. Pal recognized none from the backs of their heads, yet one thing about their features seemed distinctly obvious. The blonde and he spoke the finding simultaneously, "They're children." A moment later, sparks flew from the controls, and camera one's feed cut out. "Damn," Pal said again.

The curse was echoed in the center of the room. An alarm squealed once, then disappeared. "Four penetrations of the terrace gardens."

Chief of Security Xavian appeared then, with Delszaki Li hovering behind him.

Shintaris dashed over to report the situation.

Pal's lungs felt wrung out. "There's no way they can get through the gardens." He forced himself to sound confident, though scant moments before he would have believed the peripheral defenses nearly as secure.

"Prepare for an out force," Chief Xavian commanded, his calm voice a welcome change. "Sonar, trip beams, terrace lasers?"

Pal glanced at the indicated monitors. "Functional," he informed the chief. "And the night vids are up and going. Nothing, yet."

Several men and women vacated their seats, zipping on lightweight bevelar reflective body armor used for nothing but drills since its purchase five years earlier.

Pal walked to Shintaris and Li. "Watch the record from number one. They look like children."

Dashing to help Xavian, Shintaris accepted Pal's assessment without bothering to confirm it personally. "A ruse. They're trying to get us to drop our guard. There's got to be a full invasion force behind them." He considered as he moved, then called over his shoulder. "Most likely, the adults are the terrace breachers."

Pal brought up the map grid on his screen, its flashing notations marking the breaches. Three of the garden breaks bunched together, the fourth on the opposite side.

Chief Xavian directed the out force, hesitating as he, too, noticed the disparity.

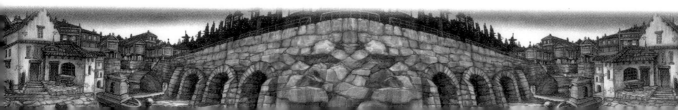

"Twelve on the three, four on the one?" His usual commanding voice petered into a hesitant question.

"Best," Shintaris said.

Pal understood the dilemma. Clearly, they were dealing with a clever adversary who divided his infiltrating troops to draw Li's security into confusion or danger. The three breaches could represent one man apiece, willing sacrifices to allow a group at position four to overpower the dwindled force protecting the single breach. It was a strategy designed to freeze them into indecision.

"Eight and eight," Xavian finally decided, allowing Shintaris to determine the specifics of each division.

Pal tapped his chair-arm console, bringing in the night cameras from the terrace gardens. The first appeared as a square in the upper left corner, the others joining it in neat rows, until his screen filled with twelve distinct vids, flowing seamlessly together. Each showed a portion of neatly tended flower beds hemmed by fences. Tight-budded, pink roses gave way to amber-petaled flowers with bulbous, scarlet centers and leaves with a gold scalloping that looked embro dered. Shaggy corelinths wove between the beds like multicolored lace. Giant sunflowers towered over the others, their seeds covered with a fine fur of pollen and their orange petals pointing crisply toward the moon. The sonar, trip-beam lasers, and vid links, some geared to darkness and others to day, lay hidden amidst the foliage, invisible. Wind tossed plant stems and heads, each movement riveting Pal's attention.

The out force was accepting its final instructions when an irregular ring of smoke

seeped along the edges of the garden. "What the hell…?" Pal stood without realizing he had moved, bending to keep his fingers on the console and his eyes glued to the screen.

"Sonar's out!" shouted a tiny man toward the middle of the room, in chorus with three others. He finished with, "High-pitched frequency. Burned out the audio pickups."

As if to confirm his words, red lights flashed over the monitoring room, the klaxons already squelched. A moment later, blinding white lights strobed the gardens, blooming out the night-vision cameras. Pal's screen blanked. The blind silence that followed was replete with terror. Sweat dribbled beneath his robe, tickling his neck. "Oh, no," he said.

Shintaris' loud curses drowned out softer ones from every part of the room. "Go!" he shouted to the out force.

Xavian dashed to the screens. "Open the floods!" he commanded, a second before Pal could do the same. The bright overhead lighting would bring the day cameras on line.

Conversation exploded in every part of the room, rife with swearing.

"One breach!" A heavyset woman leapt up and down, waving an arm to be heard over the noise. "Inner gate."

No! Disbelief preceded comprehension. *Impossible.* Pal's neck ached from his odd position, but lurches of adrenaline would not allow

him to sit. The floods snapped on, illuminating the gardens like day, just in time to pinpoint a set of skinny legs disappearing over the inner gate. "Another kid."

A mixture of comments suffused the room, ranging from simple "there"s accompanied by fingers jabbed at vid screens, to detailed descriptions, to conjecture about the intruder's intentions.

"Quiet," Chief Xavian said, the low-volumed but firm command immediately answered with silence. "Shintaris, reroute the out force.

The assistant chief scrambled to obey, catching the security team as they shot through the doorway. Surely, the massed invaders gathered by the main gate would expect Li's security to chase the nearest breach, a child likely used for diversion.

The hush admitted Shintaris' directions to the out force, "You three, catch that nearest interloper. You four, find the three in the garden. Careful, and don't forget the floods. The rest of you to the main gate." He snatched up a reflective suit. "I'm coming with you."

Pal saw Xavian nod without turning. Surely neither of the commanders could see one another, yet the chief still felt the need to show approval for Shintaris' decision.

Despite the urgency of the situation, Pal could not resist a smile. As different as their

methods and manners seemed, the two worked well together, another example of Li's shrewd ability to delegate. The wasting disease that destroyed his muscles had no influence over his brain, evidenced as much by his astute decisions as the wisdom radiating from his dark eyes.

Li rode his hover-chair to a position near Pal's left hand. "Persistent."

"And competent," Pal added, bringing up the area directly around the mansion on a series of ten cameras. "I never would have believed it possible." In Li's calming presence, Pal managed to sit, though he could not help fidgeting in the chair.

"Perhaps we should prepare to greet them."

Pal looked up, knowing he should accompany his charge, yet loathe to leave the action in the monitoring room. Resigned, he rose, only to feel Li's shriveled right hand on his shoulder. "You stay here. The servants and in-house security can handle things well enough."

Pal knew he should object but managed only, "Thank you, sir."

The gentle hiss of Li's hover-chair waned. Pal glanced over in time to see it disappear around a corner. Again, torn between remaining at Li's side and helping oversee security, he hesitated. Then, a movement on camera four fully seized his attention. A girl swaddled in a black bodywrap and hood dashed toward the mansion.

"Number seven!" Pal shouted, not alone. He hammered the zoom, dragging in a clear picture of the child, just as another bank of warning lights joined the others blazing through the room. Wisps of brown hair escaped the hood, fluttering around a button nose and a soft face blemished by linear scars across the left cheek and eye socket.

A tech hollered the obvious, "House security breach!"

"Single female child," Chief Xavian confirmed to the monitors as well as Shintaris and the out force. Black irises scarcely differentiable from the pupils focused on Albanoric's screen. "South side of the house."

The figure on the vid glanced about nervously. Then, her hands settled against steel and brick. All of the discomfort seemed to drain from her as she climbed with fluid assurance. Her fingers wedged into imperceptible irregularities, and the toes of pliable shoes followed. With the grace of an acrobat, she scrambled swiftly and steadily upward.

"Louis," Xavian said. Leaning over Albanoric, his dark fingers skittered over the console.

An elderly man answered from the corner. "She's only triggering the vibration sensors. No metal and no synthetics. No chemical adhesives."

The chief communicated with the out force. "Climbing the wall on her own power. She's alone." He tapped off-screen with a

curse of realization that triggered Pal to a similar understanding. The rooftop defenses were designed to handle helio-skimmers and space skiffs, but the weight of a small child could not possibly activate them. Pal found himself torn between worry and relief. No matter who the child worked for, he wished no harm upon her; nor could they tolerate her trespass.

Xavian finished with a warning. "Avoid deadly force if at all possible."

The input from camera seven returned to walls and plants as the girl clambered beyond its range. Pal tapped back to the broad view of the inner circle, assuring with a glance that others studied the terrace gardens, walls, main gate, and map grid. All seemed quiet, except for visions of the out force, Shintaris at the head, charging down the slope to confront the invasion force. Pal shivered. The missing inputs could hide anything.

A metallic voice snapped over Chief Xavian's audio. "She's on the roof, sir."

"Spread out," Xavian commanded. "Prepare for a window breach." He informed the out force and the monitoring room simultaneously.

"At once, sir," the other returned from the audio.

Abrupt dread seized Pal. *Acorna!*

Shintaris' voice snapped over the audio next. "No one here, chief. Main gate's deserted." He added carefully, "Control panel's professionally damaged."

"Keep looking. Spread out, if you need to, but close your contact."

"Yes, sir."

Pal dashed for the doorway, halted by Xavian's command. "Kendoro, alert the inside. Inform Li. Make certain no one's caught unaware by a sudden presence through a window."

"At once," Pal returned hurriedly, snatching up a hand-held audio left by the out force. Concern drove him to run to Acorna first, but no one could set the chain of events into motion with his skill. He needed to inform the head servants and Delszaki Li first. Sprinting through the doorway, he set to his task.

Shortly after crawling into bed, Acorna had found sleep impossible, her mind returning determinedly to the frightened, young girl who Gill and Rafik had rescued from Didi Badini's brothel. Acorna had crept from her own room to the girl's, finding the child huddled in a fetal position, tears gliding down her cheeks. Though warring with exhaustion, fear had kept sleep at bay for the girl as well.

Hours later, a sound awakened Acorna. She opened her eyes, muscle cramps trickling into awareness. She lay sprawled at the girl's bedside, her legs and torso on the floor, her arms propped against the mattress and her horn locked in the girl's protective fist. Acorna

levered her horn free without awakening the child. She cocked her head, ears flicking to catch the noise that had awakened her. Silver eyes scanned the room, instantly catching a slight movement of the door.

Acorna rose silently as the panel edged open on well-oiled hinges. A brown eye peeked through the crack, accompanied by a quarter of a child's face and a shaggy clump of chestnut hair. Acorna recognized him at once. "Sanga!"

The boy's eyes rolled upward, and he mouthed words of relief. Stepping inside, he pulled the door shut behind him. "Not so loud, please, Sita Ram." He crept toward her, eyes never still.

"You're safe here," Acorna said, the girl stirring as she spoke.

"Not safe," Sanga sidled to the window, glancing out the glass with the same caution with which he had entered the room. "I sneaked past security."

Only then it occurred to Acorna that Pal had proudly deemed the Li mansion impenetrable. "How did you get here?"

Sanga slid behind a floor length curtain, its silky fabric clinging to his tattered kameez. "I had help. Some of the kids worked in factories that built these security gadgets. They created a diversion. I waited till servants came out to make repairs, then slipped in the door behind them." He shook his head fiercely. "I came to deliver a message. Then I've got to get out."

"Listen…," Acorna started, interrupted by a tap on the door that awakened the girl. She jerked to a sitting position, eyes wild. Sanga studied the windows frantically. "Behind the curtain," Acorna whispered. "I won't give you away." She turned the girl a meaningful look intended to keep her silent as well, then called to the door. "Who is it?" By the time she returned her gaze to Sanga, he had disappeared amid the curtain's folds.

The door whisked open to admit Pal Kendoro. "Acorna, thank goodness you're here. There's been a security breach. When I didn't find you in your room—"

Xavian's voice stabbed over the radio. "Pal, the girl just ran across the roof, then came straight down. Weren't expecting that. They're in pursuit."

"Excuse me," Pal told Acorna and the girl before addressing Xavian. "Better check for sabotage."

"Nothing." Xavian had obviously already done so. "Sensors are intact. If she left anything, it's not metal, synthetic, poison, explosive, or living. Nguyen's headed up there now."

Pal studied Acorna, still speaking through the radio. "Has Shintaris found anything?"

"Nothing but the damage we already knew about."

Pal headed for the window.

Acorna sucked in a sharp breath.

Pal glanced toward her. "What's wrong?"

"Nothing," Acorna said, hating herself for lying to a loved one…again. "What are you doing?"

"Making sure the latches are secured." Pal drew directly to the window, his right leg touching the child bundled behind the curtain. Apparently satisfied, he stepped back. "You look nervous. Do you want me to stay with you till this blows over?"

"No." Acorna tried to sound reassuring rather than anxious, with some success. "I'm fine. They need you."

Pal nodded uncertainly, black hair uncharacteristically disheveled and, she could not help noticing, rather attractive. "All right. But I'll be back to check on you in a bit."

"Fine," Acorna said. "Thank you."

Pal gave her another once over. "You're sure?"

"Of course, I'm sure." Acorna managed a smile. She waved him away with a white-furred arm. "Go do what you have to do."

Pal lowered his head in a gesture more bow than nod. He headed from the room, closing the door behind him.

Several moments passed in silence. Acorna listened for signs that Pal was returning, hearing only his dwindling footsteps. "It's safe," she told Sanga.

The boy's head thrust from the curtains, its fabric draped like neo-Hadithian veils. "Safe," he said, "is a relative term."

Acorna smiled, impressed by his vocabulary as well as his sense of humor. Those most dependent upon Kezdet's bonded labor system had sabotaged schools created for the children, worried that their slave-like work gangs would learn to calculate their so-called wages and the amounts needed to buy off their contracts. Sanga's verbal agility suggested he had managed some education, probably before greedy or overburdened relatives had sold him into Kezdet's service. "I sent Pal away because I promised I would, but he's not a danger to you. Any time you want to see me, you need only ring the main gate."

The girl pulled the covers around her, propped on an elbow. Tangled mahogany hair draped to her shoulders. "Don't worry for Lukia. She and her friends is all nice. I should know."

Sanga wrung his hands, head swinging in every direction. "I don't have time to chat. Please, let me speak my piece and leave."

Acorna wished for the words to make Sanga understand. For the moment, she knew, he would not pay attention to her until she fully gained his trust by allowing him control of the situation. "I'm listening," she assured.

Sanga relaxed notably, though his gaze still sketched arcs, seeking danger. "The Dodger wants you to meet with him tonight. He said you have to come alone."

Acorna frowned, pupils narrowing. She shook back her silver mane of hair. "Alone?"

"Alone," Sanga repeated. "If you bring others, you won't find him." He drew a crumpled piece of paper from his pocket and handed it to Acorna.

She smoothed the scrap between single-jointed fingers, then studied the crude map of East Celtalan. A route on the main streets was marked, ending in an "X" that clearly indicated the meeting site.

Sanga next pulled an electronic device from his pocket, running it over the latches on the window, recently checked by Pal. Lights flickered through a spectrum that made Sanga frown.

Acorna touched his arm. "Even if I could sneak out of here without getting caught, it wouldn't be fair to my friends. I promised I wouldn't place myself in danger again without discussing it with them first."

Sanga turned his head to Acorna. "Dodger didn't say anything about not telling anyone, just that you had to come alone."

Acorna considered the loophole as Sanga worked on the locks. The first one clicked, and he stiffened before starting on the second. "Sanga, listen. We've rescued most of Kezdet's children from intolerable situations and have given them a safe haven on Maganos." The second lock clicked, and he slid the window open. "We can do the same for you and your friends."

The boy indicated the window with a jerk of his thumb. "I disabled the locks and defenses, but not the alarms. In a moment, security will come." He scrambled to the ledge.

Afraid to lose another chance to rescue the children from a life of forced theft, she continued swiftly. "Sanga, think about it. And let the others know. Any child who wants a better life need only come out where we can find him or her."

Sanga scurried out the window, his last soft words hanging on the air. "Thank you, Sita Ram. But I'm happy here."

Shocked by words Acorna had never heard from the lips of a child on Kezdet, she stood in wonderment for several moments.

The slam of footsteps in the hallway and a steady wash of warm air through the window drew Acorna from her trance. The door zipped open, and a half dozen men and women hammered inside, led by Pal. The girl flinched beneath the covers. Acorna whirled.

"Is everything all right?" Pal asked.

"Fine," Acorna insisted. "Just needed some air."

Pal rolled his eyes, waving the others away. Exchanging grins, the men and women dispersed. The girl peeked from the dark cave of her blankets.

As the door clicked closed behind them, Acorna resorted to the truth Pal deserved. "I did need some air. But that's not why the window's open."

Pal turned as if to call the others back; then, something in Acorna's expression stopped him. He walked to her. "What's going on?"

"A child was here," she explained, prepared to stop him if he activated the radio.

"Where?" Pal spun, eyes as active as Sanga's had been.

"He's gone now." Acorna took Pal's hand and pulled him to the floor beside her. "He just wanted to tell me something." Anticipating his next question, she added, "The Dodger sent him."

"The Dodger." Pal pursed his lips. Her words explained much. "Damn," he whispered with obvious anger. The heel of his hand banged the side of his head. "I should have thought of that." He hit himself again. "Stupid." He started to rise, but Acorna pulled him back down.

"Why should you have thought of that?" she asked, tone soothing, not demanding. "We haven't made contact with him. Gill and Rafik tried, but not Mr. Li. Or you. Or me."

Pal settled back into place, draping an arm across her shoulders. "Gill and Rafik were enough, Sweetie," he said. "And we've made electronic inquiries." He lapsed into thoughtful silence before repeating the curse, this time sounding more impressed than annoyed. His lids drooped, leaving only slits. "The Dodger orchestrated…that…" The word encompassed a depth of meaning Acorna could not guess. "…to deliver a message."

Growing braver, the girl sat up in bed, head no longer hidden. She kept the blanket wrapped tightly around her, understandably more uncomfortable around men than women.

"Well, that explains the kids." Pal's eyes widened back to normal, revealing the familiar dark and gentle eyes. "Now, what message was worth all that trouble?"

"He wants a meeting."

Pal's features brightened, and he turned Acorna a smile. "That's great! When? Where? Did he say how to contact him? Did he—"

"Whoa." Acorna pressed her fingers to Pal's knee. "Let me answer before you ask another question." She tried to recall his interrogatives in order. "Yes, it's great. Tonight after dusk." She placed the map in his lap. "Here, I believe." She pointed to the X on the document. "And no."

"No?"

Acorna grinned back. "No, Sanga didn't say how to contact him."

"Sanga?"

"The same boy who rescued me from the brothel."

"Which confirms that the message actually came from the Dodger." Pal shifted to a crouch, removing his arm from Acorna. "We need to discuss this with Rafik and Gill. Make some plans before we go."

Apparently tiring of the discussion, the girl settled back onto her pillow, snuggling beneath the blankets.

Acorna braced for Pal's wrath. "There is no 'we', Pal. If I don't come alone, he won't meet me."

"No," Pal said. Though neither sharp nor harsh, the syllable carried authority.

Acorna stroked Pal's soft hair. "Think of the children."

Without intention, Pal leaned into her touch. "I am thinking of the children. Like this one." He gestured at the girl whose lids wilted despite the noise of their conversation. "And the hundreds on Maganos. What would they do without you?"

His words struck a painful chord. "They'll have you. Gill and Judit. And all the others who have helped organize and teach, good people who have dedicated their lives to this project." Her fingers stilled on his head, and she looked deeply into his eyes. "It's no different than if I returned to my home planet, if Calum finds it."

82

Pal stared back, granting no quarter. He turned Acorna to face him directly. "It's different," he asserted. "It's completely different. Death and departure?" He shook his head. "How can you compare them?"

Surely, he knew the answer, but Acorna dutifully explained. "Either way, I'm gone."

"But one way, you're dead!" Pal flapped a hand, briskly dismissing. "It's senseless arguing. The only thing that matters is you're not going alone."

Acorna gathered a foot under her just so she could stomp it. "Pal, stop it! When did you become the sole decision-maker for me?"

Pal sucked in a deep breath, then let it out slowly. He lowered his head. "I'm sorry, Acorna. You're right. I'm just keyed up from the break-in: still in loud, commanding, action mode. Of course, you have a say in this. And Gill and Rafik do, too. And Mr. Li, if he's allowed to conjecture, will certainly deliver a wise and rational recommendation." He slumped, looking nearly defeated.

Having never seen Pal so discouraged, Acorna embraced him, nuzzling his bangs with her horn, trying to lift his spirits. "It'll work out, Pal. One way or another. I'm sure the others will find a way to save the meeting without placing me in too much danger."

Pal returned the hug, patting Acorna on the back. "I know it'll work out. I'm just physically and emotionally wrung out, thrown into a tense situation on very little sleep. If I'd thought before speaking, I'd have realized that the Dodger could have sent an assassin instead of a messenger." He kissed her cheek and managed a feeble smile. "One thing for certain, if this meeting happens, promise me you'll ask how in the universe he managed that siege."

Acorna grinned back. "I promise."

Dawnlight funneled through casement windows, playing across mismatched couches, chairs and grimy bedding spread across the floor. Spirals of white padding and an occasional spring jutted from fraying holes in the upholstery, the patches unable to keep up with wear. His back against the farthest corner, the Dodger propped a tattered copy of Charles Dickens's *Oliver Twist* on his knees. Though ancient and antiquated, it was his favorite story and the one from which he had taken his name. Children spread through the room, in various stages of repose, each with a book or bound manuscript hardcopy from the library. He had insisted that those not out working performed their studies, as usual, yet, found himself unable to concentrate. Until Sanga, Jevic, and the others returned safely, he could not help worrying for them.

An unruly mop of bronze hair with just a hint of curl fell across the Dodger's high forehead,

missing the steely eyes only because of the deliberate patch he had hacked from the center. From the day he had escaped Kezdet's bonded labor system, he had savored every moment of leisure, particularly his time curled with a precious book. His thoughts glided back to his early years, when schools had still existed there. The memories remained vivid, preciously preserved. Those few months had brought so much knowledge that even exhaustion and pain would never force him to forget details that had saved his life on more than one occasion. *I would never have known about the antibiotics that saved my toes.* The Dodger glanced toward his feet, bare, as usual. Striped and deformed by scars, they swelled painfully whenever he wore shoes for longer than a couple hours or when the need for supplies forced him to excessive activity. In the past several years, the children had made those forays less and less necessary.

Where are they? Worry drove the Dodger to pace, but long years of forcing composure kept him in place. If the readers saw him fretting, they would become distressed; and he wanted to spare them a concern that was, for the time being, his alone. *If I got even one of them killed, I'll never forgive myself.* In the twelve years he had spent collecting and succoring Kezdet's abandoned children, he had lost some to illnesses or injuries that he could not gather the

supplies or expertise to heal. But never had a child died on a mission for him. *Where are they?*

As if in answer, a solid series of knocks, in the proper sequence, banged through the room. The Dodger jerked to his feet, yet Charlas bounded to the door ahead of him. Peering through the peephole, she reported. "It's them."

Thank goodness. The Dodger resettled his spare, sinewy frame into his corner. He shook the sandy-brown tangles from his broad shoulders as Charlas flung the panel open and the children sent to the Li mansion returned. His gray gaze flickered over the group, seeking injuries he did not find. Only then, his broad lips twitched into a smile. "How'd it go?"

"Breeze," Sanga said, as always. Sweat leached through his shirt, and streaks of moss stained his pants. Twigs twined through his red-brown hair.

Jevic turned to him with a wide-mouthed glare, her bodywrap torn and filthy. "Speak for youself, Breezy. You dint hafta lead a s'cur'ty team on a chase."

The Dodger knew Sanga greatly understated his own trials, but nothing he or the others could say would get the boy to admit the difficulty. Compared to life in Kezdet's mines, no task of the Dodger's seemed anything but a pleasant challenge to Sanga. The older man understood his charge's attitude, even shared it. He, too, had

escaped the mines and a cruel master who had ruined his feet and riddled his body with whip scars. Even in his worst days of aching he reveled in his freedom, eternally happy. Yet, now, something threatened that happiness. And that something bore the name Acorna.

"Message delivered," Sanga said cheerfully.

"Great." The Dodger smiled at each of the eight in turn, then clapped a hand to Sanga's shoulder to display his pride.

The children fairly glowed. Unaccustomed to praise, they thrived in it, though a too effusive delivery would make them more embarrassed and suspicious than honored.

The Dodger executed an arcing gesture. "Get some sleep. Everyone. I'll need you all at main stations this afternoon."

The children rushed to obey, some skittering from the backs, arms, and seats of furniture while others glued their attention to their stories, seeking chapter ends or scene breaks before putting the manuscripts gingerly aside. Though cleaning ranked last place in his priorities, he instilled his respect for books into every child who joined his gang.

The Dodger found a quiet corner while the children lined up at the sink or prepared themselves for bed. A few planted themselves near doors or windows or slipped out into the streets. These had rested the night, and were now wide awake for the day time, watching for

events in East Celtalan and keeping the Dodger, his charges, and his secrets safe.

Sanga drifted to the Dodger, who absently hugged him like a father. "A breeze, huh?"

Sanga smiled.

"Anything I need to know about?" The Dodger released the boy.

Sanga played his gaze over his leader's prominent, well-shaped nose and close but deep-set eyes. "She asked me to go with her to Maganos."

The Dodger stifled a reaction, though his throat felt constricted. From long habit, he managed to maintain an unemotional mask. "Oh?" The word emerged higher pitched than he intended, more question than expression of understanding. Betrayed by his own voice, the Dodger continued with the necessary question. "What did you tell her?" He could feel his heart quicken in his chest, the response more significant than Sanga could ever know.

Sanga's dark eyes revealed nothing. "What did you want me to say?"

That we're a family. That you love us too much to consider leaving. The Dodger's hands balled to fists. *That you're insulted at the bare mention of such a thing.* But he did not say those things—he could not. An ancient Earth expression came to him then: *If you love something, let it go.* He lowered his head, hair

falling along defined cheekbones and his chiseled chin sinking to his chest. "I'd miss you terribly. But I hope you followed your heart and chose what was best for you."

"I did." Sanga's look and tone still gave away nothing, and the Dodger cursed himself for that. The boy had learned that perfect lack of expression from him.

The Dodger's fingers loosened, and his brow gradually rose in question.

Sanga stopped torturing his mentor. "I told her I was happy here." He grinned. "And I am." A moment later, his features knitted, no trace of the smile remaining. "What's right for me isn't necessarily right for the others."

The Dodger found maintaining eye contact almost impossible. "I've never kept anyone against their will. I don't plan to start, now." *If you love something....* He clamped down on the thought. *Once Acorna's dead, it won't matter.*

"Is that why you're meeting with her?"

Now, the Dodger had to look away. He turned the need into a careful sweep of the room to assure that no one overheard them. Engrossed in their own conversations, the children washed and readied themselves for sleep. Several already snuggled into the ragged blankets on the floor or on various couches and chairs. Hannoh pulled the curtains over the casements, plunging the room into a dank grayness. "Yes," he said, hating himself for the necessary lie. Better for all of them if the children never knew about his indirect role in Acorna's murder. "I need to understand what she's offering and decide whether I trust her before I present the option to the gang." He indicated everyone in the room with a spiraling movement of his arm.

Sanga rubbed small hands, expression growing soft, almost distant. "She's wonderful, Dodger."

The Dodger suffered a pang suspiciously akin to jealousy. He refused to discard Sanga's assessment, yet he could not afford to accept it out of hand. "Then I'll find her so, too. But I've spent too long scratching gilded layers off brass not to check things out for myself." He turned Sanga a pointed look. "I want what's best for those I care for. I want them to make educated decisions. You understand, don't you?"

"Of course, I understand." This time Sanga initiated the embrace.

The Dodger held Sanga, feeling both closer and further from the boy than ever in the past. It pained him that such fellowship was tainted with deceit for the first time.

❁　　❁　　❁

Curled on a carpet remnant near the hideaway's sequestered door, the Dodger found himself unable to sleep. Repeatedly, thoughts paraded through his mind, ranging from a desperate guilt to a grim certainty that he had chosen the only possible course. Acorna, not he, had forced the issue. Lacking the inside knowledge necessary to rescue all of Kezdet's children, she would always leave some behind to face the indecent fate the labor system inflicted upon them. He had found the ones she missed, had turned them from unwanted orphans and near-corpses to self-confident members of a decidedly non-traditional, but no less loving, family. *I can't let her take that away.*

For the ninetieth time, the Dodger rolled, seeking a comfort that escaped him. No new position could rescue him from his own uncomfortable thoughts. The glow in Sanga's eyes when he spoke of Acorna haunted the Dodger even into the shallow sleep he finally managed, and the boy's words seemed to echo in his head: "She asked me to go with her to Maganos." *To Maganos. To Maganos.* Suddenly, Kezdet's primary moon, so long a welcome staple in the sky, became an object of dire loathing. *Unwelcome bitch!* The idea came, accompanied by a rush of fiery loathing. *I hate you!* Hot tears burned the Dodger's eyes, the first ones he could recall in longer than a decade. The cold tears he shed over the dead and dying bore little resemblance to these.

The Dodger rolled again. Seeking elusive respite, he turned his thoughts toward a topic he had so many times deliberately slammed to the deepest recesses of his mind. The details of the tragedy in the Gorag mines returned in horrific detail. Even time could not soften events so indelibly etched on his memory.

The deafening whine of the compressors filled the dark tunnels, and rock splinters slashed and hammered exposed flesh. It had taken only a glimpse of Carloy's blood-smeared face, his cheek gaping in a long flap as Finan Telmark hauled him screaming from Below, to convince the Dodger to always keep the shielding mask over his face. He had never seen Carloy again, but the rivulets of blood haunted his dreams for years afterward. The ventilation fans kept the stench of the mines partially at bay, and familiarity handled what the fans left behind.

The Dodger had outgrown his shoes the same year that vandalism and violence closed Kezdet's schools for the laborers. His life became an endless cycle of darkness and light, Below and Above, the sting of rock chips while hewing ore from cave faces and the blessed relief of a sleep that exhaustion rendered as quiet as death. Only the dreams of Carloy's blood, half-formed remembrances of nurturing parents lost to an accident, and passages of cherished books penetrated those hours of peace. And, as evening descended upon the world, Finan Telmark's kicks and curses had turned to whip strokes if he did not awaken swiftly enough. It had taught him to sleep on the barest edge of awakening, a skill that had served him well in later years on the streets.

For that alone, he owed his former master a debt of gratitude, one he would revel in paying back—with a laser blast through the gut.

Bare feet fared poorly on gallery floors plated with hunks of rough-hewn rock, especially in a darkness the lamps scarcely penetrated. The cuts and abrasions on his limbs seemed insignificant compared to the agony of his unprotected feet. Infection followed infection. His soles and toes intermittently leaked a red-tinged pus that he hid beneath the ragged scraps of his outgrown kameezes. If Finan Telmark discovered the ailment, the Dodger would disappear as Carloy did, to a fate he dared not contemplate. Those removed from the work gang for sickness or injury were not handled gently and never, ever returned.

The night had started as every other. Shortly after dusk, he, Yvair, Deven, and Rethwix had huddled in the cage as it plummeted into the depths of the underground tunnels, slamming the rock floor with an impact that lost all four their footing. Deven loosed a harsh curse, shaking a dark fist at the inattentive minder. Yvair tripped the latch, butted the door with his head and crawled into the tunnel without bothering to stand. His blond head bobbed through the darkness, and pale, gawky limbs jutted from a kameez whose color became swallowed in the

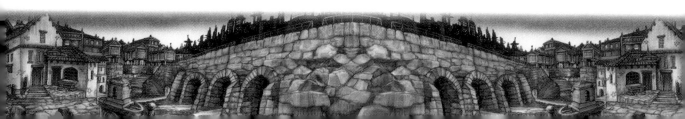

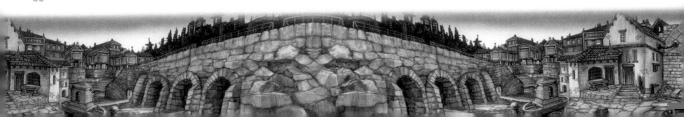

gloom. The eldest, sixteen-year-old Rethwix, stood the shortest of them all, barely needing to stoop as he hauled out a lantern and followed Yvair. Deven and the Dodger, then called by his given name, Taison, followed.

The four hewers picked their way cautiously to their assignment, Face One. The Dodger's feet ached worse than usual, and every step onto the uneven surface sent a fresh stab of agony through them. He lagged, biting his lip against pain, unwilling to share the affliction even with his companions. Any weakness became a danger the others might hold over him in times of strife or accidently reveal to Finan Telmark in a crazed moment of pain or utter fatigue.

"Taison, keep up!" Rethwix shouted, though how the older boy saw him tarrying in the dark tunnel slanting toward Face One, with Deven between them, the Dodger did not try to guess. He simply quickened his pace, as aware as any of them that not making their allotment might result in a beating for all of them. His hand drifted to the whip cut that scarred his left shoulder, the anguish of his feet momentarily forgotten.

The empty corves they would soon top with ore stood like silent shadows in the gloom. Worried for the day's production on an unyielding rock face that surrendered its ore with uncharacteristic reluctance, the others ran to their stations. Worried that he would carry the

blame alone should output fall below quota, the Dodger scurried after them. The ball of his foot smashed down on a sharp edge of rock as the first compressor whirred to life. Agony lanced through his entire leg, and a white bolt of light stole even dark-vision. Beyond thought, he collapsed, rolling beneath a corf. A moment later a loud crack hammered his hearing, carrying the dangerous finality of a tree on the verge of falling. Then, the gallery seemed to shudder, and a mass of rock avalanched from the roof.

The sudden realization of death slammed the Dodger as tons of rock drummed into the corf above his head. Ducking behind the wheels, he searched frantically for his companions. Screams melded with the crash and thud of heavy stones. Catching sight of Yvair's ivory legs through the gap, the Dodger lunged into harm's way without thought. A boulder bashed against his shoulder, but desperate need swallowed his pain. Seizing the legs of his terror-paralyzed companion, the Dodger hauled him beneath the corf while stones struck the area above and around them. Then, as suddenly as the cave-in started, it stopped.

The Dodger choked in a breath saturated with dust, then coughed in hacking paroxysms until moisture blurred his vision and his lungs cleared. He spat out a mouthful of dirt-speckled sputum and tiny rock shards before finally turning his attention to his companion. "Yvair?"

The blonde lay still, unmoving.

Terror clutched the Dodger's heart. "Yvair?" He shook the boy, thirteen years old, the same age as himself. The thought seemed unimportant, yet, it would not leave his head. "Yvair!" Concern for the others followed. "Rethwix! Deven!" *I'm alone.* He fought panic. "Rethwix!"

A faint voice answered from further down the tunnel, Deven's the Dodger believed. "I'm here."

The Dodger scrambled toward the sound, banging his head on the underside of the corf. He sank to the floor.

Yvair moaned. His head jerked, revealing a trickle of blood from his right ear and a sticky patch of dirty scarlet plastering the hair to that side of his head.

Torn between two needy friends, the Dodger hesitated. Carefully, he attempted to ease the corf from over himself and Yvair, but the wheeled cart would not budge. Lowering his head, he wriggled from beneath it, unprepared for the carnage that confronted him. To his left, rock sealed the tunnel, floor to ceiling. Deven's call had come from beyond there, and it seemed a miracle that the Dodger had heard the boy at all. All around, rock lay heaped in sloping, unsteady piles. To his right, the wall of rock rose to just above his head. He believed he could scale it and scramble to freedom. For the moment, however, his friends' lives took precedence.

"Deven?" the Dodger shouted.

No answer.

More desperate, now: "Deven!"

The faint trickle of the ten-year-old's voice wafted to him, a shout muffled nearly to a whisper. "I'm here." No question now that it came from deeper in the gallery. "Yvair?"

"Taison." The Dodger stared at the landslide rampart that separated him from his companion, refusing to allow the hopelessness of the task to penetrate. "I'll get you out," he promised loudly. "You're going to be all right." Once spoken, the words became a certainty he dared not question. Grasping the first bit of rubble blocking his way to the wall, he shoved it behind him. A second boulder followed, then he wrestled with a third. "Is Rethwix with you?"

No reply came from the behind the rocks. "Deven?"

"No!" the younger boy shouted, probably for the second time.

Where the hell? The Dodger tried not to contemplate. He set to moving the rubble at the fastest possible pace. "Can you dig out from your side?"

A brief pause ensued, followed by a lament that shifted in and out of hearing volume. "No ... surrounded ... large stones ... space you couldn't even fit ... could move would ... crushed ... any of ... shifted."

The Dodger forced away the image of cramped

darkness, not daring to move for fear of causing one's own death. "I'll get you out. I promise."

An hour passed before the Dodger cleared a space just to reach the main pile, and conversation disappeared as his breath emerged in wheezing pants. He looked at the floor to ceiling wall again, shaking back hair that oozed sweat. This time, he could not keep realization at bay. *It'd take machines to get him out.* No child, he knew, was worth that kind of money to Finan Telmark.

Dropping back on his heels, the Dodger suffered his first moments of despair. Tears gathered in his eyes, and the pains he had managed to keep at bay assailed him simultaneously. His shoulder ached deep in its socket; every movement jangled sharp anguish through it. Agony pulsed through his feet, and he now noticed the patches of pus-thickened blood smeared across several stones. He sank to the floor, overcome by a sudden rush of hopelessness that rendered him incapable of movement.

The Dodger lay there, still and silent, when scraping noises and exchanged bursts of indecipherable conversation reached his ears. These stopped suddenly, replaced by urgent calls. Then, Finan Telmark's voice rose over the others, initially a broad range of raucous swearing. The children remained silent as he defined their new assignments: "Brusni, you're dragging for Face Three. Meezir, you'll have to help Troy trap for Face Six. Hakir, you take…" His voice faded as they headed away from the avalanche and the boys trapped behind it.

Help! The Dodger tried to cry out, but his throat refused to work. *Help Deven. Help Yvair.* He swallowed, fighting his vocal cords. *Help…me.*

Someone in the back sobbed, surely for the fate of the hewers. The Dodger thought he heard his name before Finan Telmark's unintelligible reply ended any further discussion.

Logic ended the struggle as the voices and footsteps faded. The Dodger looked at his tattered, contaminated feet. If Finan Telmark found him, the gang master would dump him in whatever incinerator claimed the bodies of unproductive children, leaving Deven, Rethwix, and Yvair to die. Closing his mouth, the Dodger stopped attempting to call and forced himself to stand.

Six more hours of shifting stone brought the Dodger to a state of exhaustion beyond that of any working day. His shoulder hurt so much that every movement became a struggle. His feet had gone numb, and his eyelids fought to close. Even envisioning Deven's situation failed to bring him the second wind it had earlier, and he lacked the energy to verbally check on his friend. Blurry-eyed, he glanced at the wall of stone. For every rock he had moved, it seemed another shifted to take its place. As far as he could tell, he had accomplished nothing other than to increase the rubble surrounding himself.

Yvair came to him then, dazed and shaky. "I want to help," he said, voice hoarse.

The Dodger did not have the strength to refuse him. Together, they heaved at a massive boulder that had defied him since the start. Pain ground through his entire body as the stone first resisted, then budged ever so slightly. A moment later, it popped free, followed by a rush of blood. The Dodger caught a glimpse of crushed, swarthy fingers before the gallery rumbled again and rocks filled the gap they had created. "Rethwix," he managed to whisper before his breakfast staggered back up his esophagus. He and Yvair ran to separate corners to vomit.

The Dodger shocked awake in a familiar cold sweat he had not experienced in longer than five years. He remembered the rest: Deven's voice had grown weaker over the ensuing night, his last words unforgettable: "Taison. Yvair." Somehow, the gasping whisper from a dry mouth had managed to penetrate stone. "You can't get to me before I die. My friends, save the ones you can."

Save the ones you can. For three years, that had meant no one except himself. Then Dodger and Yvair had dragged themselves from the mines, scrambling up the cage ropes and dodging the minder's engines. Once on the streets, Yvair quickly succumbed to the aftermath of a head wound more serious than either of them had realized. Stolen antibiotic had rescued the Dodger's feet but not his conscience. *Save the ones you can.* He had dedicated the last fourteen years of his life to just that cause. The streets had taught him much, and he passed that knowledge, along with the security of numbers, the loyalty and love of a family, and his brief education to any child rescued from bonded labor or lost on Kezdet's streets.

Until Acorna came to destroy it. The hostility

inspired by that thought carried the Dodger through the rest of a mostly sleepless day until approaching evening forced him to the waiting spot he had selected. Careful to avoid Farsiri's Alley, he sent the gang to their usual chain of spying.

The reports came back almost immediately, in the grayness shortly before the approaching dusk. First, Jevic settled beside him to announce the landing of a skimmer on the far side of the bridge to East Celtalan, at the extreme edge of the Riverwalk. "Acorna's out first, headin' into the city. Then there's these two guys, one a great big redhead with a beard and the other a regular-size mister with brownish skin and black hair."

The Dodger nodded from beneath his broad-brimmed hat. He recognized the descriptions as the same two who had sought him throughout East Celtalan.

Jevic continued, "They's followin' her at a distance. Then there's these other guys what circled around. One's a tall mister with a wrap on his head and a graying beard."

The Dodger felt his chest tighten as he listened to the description of Hafiz Harakamian, a man even he would not like to meet in East Celtalan's alleys.

"The other's a Asian guy."

The Dodger knew that one, too. "Good work," he said in a low voice.

Jevic disappeared, replaced by a series of children who marked the passage of all three groups in low whispers. The pattern soon became clear. Acorna took the direct route to the designated meeting point. Rafik and Gill followed her at a distance clearly designed to allow them to get to her quickly should problems arise, yet, without interfering with their business. He did not begrudge them that security, had even anticipated it. The children would warn him if Gill or Rafik displayed any obvious weaponry or drew within striking distance, and he trusted his quickness and knowledge of the city to escape a physical attack. Their deliberate use of a single skimmer and lack of any clear intention to hide suggested that they wanted him to notice them.

Pal and Hafiz adopted a similar strategy, walking openly through East Celtalan in a broad circle that would bring them to the meeting site after the business commenced.

Sanga brought the only unrelated news. "There're two others about. A derelict who always hangs out near the corner of Contigo and Madisar. Drunk, as usual." He glanced about surreptitiously. "And a scrubby stranger in black hanging out in Farsiri's Alley." Worry marred the gentle brown of his eyes. "Looks like a pro."

The Dodger frowned, shaking off what he already knew was true. "Why would a pro be here?" The lie cut deeper than he expected,

95

and he did not give Sanga a chance to contemplate. "Just in case, tell the gang to steer wide. No one is to go near him. Clear?"

"Clear." Sanga studied his leader, as if reading something.

The Dodger scowled, hunching deeper into the shadows and pulling his hat brim further over his face.

Cloth scraped roof tiles overhead. "Dodger," Hannoh said in a loud whisper. "She's reached the far end of the street. ETA: three minutes."

Three minutes to me. Two minutes to fate. The image of a shifting stone, followed by a scarlet surge of blood filled his memory. The comparison seemed nonsensical. Lasers burned, a clean and bloodless death.

Sanga gave the Dodger's hand a brotherly squeeze. "Good luck. She's a good woman. I'm sure she'll be reasonable."

Reasonable. The Dodger contemplated his own strategy, Sanga's words from that morning returning unbidden: *"What's right for me is not necessarily what's right for the others."* And his own claim: *"I've never kept anyone against their will. I don't plan to start now."* Not then, but now. *If you love something, let it go....* Acorna came into view, a slender creature with a flowing, silver mane and a horn that seemed to glow through the enfolding darkness. He saw his gang, his family, leaning from roof ledges and peering out windows to catch a glimpse of the magnificent young woman who seemed blithely unaware of their presences or her effect upon them. Even from a distance, he read a joy in his follower's eyes that approached worship, a fondness that a thirty-year-old, damaged escapee from Kezdet's mines could never share.

Save the ones you can. And he had. Yet, the Dodger realized, if he betrayed their trust, he destroyed the very ones he claimed to have saved. As if in slow motion, he saw Acorna reach the mouth of Farsiri's Alley, felt himself darting toward her. Then, it was too late to shout warnings. Gill and Rafik would never arrive in time. Acorna's life or death lay in his hands.

I'm sorry, Sanga. The Dodger flung himself in front of Acorna, even as the first flash left Farsiri's alley. Pain boiled through his chest. He felt himself falling, as if through a vast void. Then he knew nothing more.

Unexpectedly toppled and crushed, Acorna screamed. Footsteps pounded through the alleyways as she squirmed from beneath the dead weight that pinned her. Suddenly, it shifted, and Pal's hand appeared. Accepting it, she allowed him to haul her to her feet, the Dodger's body rolling limply aside. Then she noticed several things at once. Rafik and Gill disappeared down an alley, in pursuit of someone. Hafiz towered over her. A crowd of children materialized from the shadows, innocent fairies dressed in every shade of gray and black. This once, they had not come for her.

A girl cradled the man's head, tears streaming down her cheeks. Another screamed "no" repeatedly, apparently incapable of any other sound or action, as if certain enough denial would change what had happened. Others stroked the still body, sobbing.

Tenderly, Acorna pushed them aside, finding the burns that melded the Dodger's black shirt with his skin. His hat had fallen from his head, now snuggled in a little boy's arms, spilling bronze hair across the dusty cobbles. She touched her horn to the wound with a gentle caress, her eyes silver balls with only a hint of slitted pupil.

"Acorna," Hafiz warned. "That must be the Dodger. Are you sure you want to…"

Acorna listened to nothing more. She watched as the flesh coalesced, easing free of the cloth then resuming its natural conformation. It did not matter who she healed. Anyone this loved by any child deserved her attention. One trusted by so many had earned whatever assistance she could provide. She ran her horn over ancient whip scars peeking through the tattered fabric, then touched the damaged feet. Finally, she hovered over his chest, urging the shocked heart to beat, the stunned lungs to resume their breathing.

Rafik and Gill returned, a dark-clad figure struggling between them. "We caught—" Gill broke off at the sight of the gathered children and the steel gray flicker of the Dodger's eyes that turned from startled to terrified in an instant.

The Dodger struggled to rise, foiled by a sudden rush of children hurling themselves into his arms. Their exuberance sent him staggering against a warehouse wall, his regular composure wholly lost. For the first time in seventeen years, he could not escape, and the realization defeated him.

For several seconds, no one spoke. Pinned beneath Gill, the assassin went as still as the others. Hafiz and Rafik stood over them.

The Dodger made a gesture that sent some of the children scurrying back into the alleys, though many refused to leave his side. His gaze flitted between Acorna and her companions, but he did manage a surprised glance at his feet, as well.

Pal looked at his companions, deliberately placing his back to the assassin. He pitched his voice too low for them to hear, rescuing negotiations that should have taken place anywhere but a dark alley in the worst part of town. "Mr. Li wants—" he started, interrupted by Sanga who stepped protectively in front of the Dodger.

Acorna gave the boy a happy smile of recognition.

The Dodger peeked around the wall of worried children. "What does Mr. Li want?" Only a trace of defiance remained in voice that mostly revealed resignation. "My life? My family?"

Pal began again, "Dodger, we appreciate the work you've done for Kezdet's children."

The Dodger grunted. "But you're going to take them from me, aren't you?"

Acorna studied the Dodger, impressed that he worried for the children when his own life lay at stake. Surely he believed they would turn him over to the Guardians of the Peace. The money of government officials and factory owners would see to it he did not survive his imprisonment long.

"No," Pal glanced at Acorna. "We want you to continue what you're doing. We just want the opportunity to tell those you help to escape about Maganos. Some may chose to come with us. And we all want what's best for the children."

The Dodger absently fingered the tear in his shirt, above the now fully-healed wound. He had made his position clear when he deliberately took the laser blasts for Acorna. "But you won't force anyone to leave?"

"No." Pal looked at the others, apparently making certain he had not overstepped his boundaries. "Mr. Li was very impressed with your…"

"…gang," Sanga supplied.

Pal smiled. "Actually, I meant the break-in. He wants to hire you to keep him…informed of the happenings around Kezdet." He winked conspiratorially at the children around them, "And I want to know how you did it."

Acorna rose, instantly mobbed by her own share of children.

Pal continued, "For a fee, of course. Enough to finance your operation."

The Dodger claimed his hat, habitually pulling it low over features they had already had time to memorize. He said nothing, but his stillness indicated a willingness to listen.

Pal glanced once more at Gil, Rafik, and Hafiz, apparently ascertaining that the captive assassin, now bound and gagged, could not overhear or read his lips. "That one's not going to talk." He tipped his head back to indicate the assassin. "I hope you'll make finding his client your first priority."

The Dodger shifted, the darkness swallowing everything but his hands, with which he directed a gesture of gratitude at Acorna that spoke louder than any words. A moment later, the growing gloom swallowed even his hands, and the gathered children became noticeably sparser.

Acorna looked askance at Sanga.

The boy scanned the shadows before answering. The grin returned to his lips, and he faced Acorna directly. "It's Didi Badini. The Guardians of the Peace haven't found her, yet, but she can't hide from us." His last word also made it clear where his own loyalties lay. "She seems to have at least one accomplice, and we'll trap her for you, too." The grin broadened. "It'll be a breeze."

Though Acorna wished Sanga would accompany her to Maganos, the warm contentment stealing over her made it clear that, in her heart, she knew he belonged with the Dodger. Her pupils contracted to strands as she scanned the night for him.

The Dodger's calm voice floated down from the rooftops. "You've got a deal, Pal Kendoro."

Acorna gathered the ones who had chosen to stay, drawing them into a giant embrace. She smiled warmly at the darkness. And hoped the Dodger saw.

EXCERPTS FROM

THE TRAVELER'S COMPANION

A CATALOGUE OF KNOWN WORLDS

BY LYMAN FRAKOSS

KISMET

POLITICAL DESIGNATION: INDEPENDENT
SERVICE OPERATOR
PRIMARY INDUSTRY: SERVICE
ENVIRONMENT: CLASS L

Kismet is a stop-over point for travelers in the Bendle quadrant. It offers a fully-equipped dock and repair station, complete medical facilities and a variety of food, accommodations, and entertainment. Its independent status permits it to host unrestricted gambling activities, for which it has become famous. Many wealthy gamblers vacation there, and an odd subculture has formed around the activities of the idle rich.

MAGANOS

POLITICAL DESIGNATION: SATELLITE
PRIMARY: KEZDET
PRIMARY INDUSTRY: MINING AND CHILD-REARING
ENVIRONMENT: CLASS L

Maganos is the largest of Kezdet's three mineral-rich moons. Leading corporate magnate, Delszaki Li, purchased the rights to mine these satellites from the planetary government and has since established a massive mining operation here. He hopes to prove child labor is not necessary for a successful business and to provide a haven for child laborers freed from indenture in Kezdet's planet-side mines and factories. Maganos features an ingenious and innovative installation designed by legendary lunar engineer, Martin Dehoney.

KEZDET

POLITICAL DESIGNATION: INDEPENDENT STAR SYSTEM

HABITABLE PLANETS: ONE

GOVERNING PLANET: KEZDET

PRIMARY INDUSTRY: MINING AND MANUFACTURING

ENVIRONMENT: CLASS G

Kezdet is an industrial world with drastic divisions between the rich and the poor. Indentured child labor drives its mines and factories, though such practice is formally outlawed. Recent actions taken by Delszaki Li, a prominent corporate leader, and Acorna have sparked the breakdown of this system. They have liberated thousands of children, giving them new homes at a massive mining base on Maganos, Kezdet's largest satellite. Of note to travelers: Kezdet's police force and planetary government are notoriously corrupt.

LABOUE

POLITICAL DESIGNATION: INDEPENDENT STAR SYSTEM

HABITABLE PLANETS: UNKNOWN

GOVERNING PLANET: LABOUE

PRIMARY INDUSTRY: TRADING

ENVIRONMENT: CLASS G

Laboue is home to House Harakamian, a wealthy mercantile dynasty headed by Hafiz Harakamian. The location of this planet is a closely guarded secret known only to family members of the merchant clans who dwell here. Harakamian is currently caught in a minor power struggle with rival Yukata Batsu over control of Laboue's southern continent. The planet's most prominent feature is its rich and colorful heart of commerce, the Mali Bazaar.

GRIEFEN

POLITICAL DESIGNATION: INDEPENDENT
HABITABLE PLANETS: ONE
GOVERNING PLANET: GRIEFEN
PRIMARY INDUSTRY: COMMERCIAL MANUFACTURING
ENVIRONMENT: CLASS G

Griefen supports a modern society built on the wealth of a planet and solar system rich in resources. It has prospered by processing abundant raw materials into products for export. The planetary government is currently building a series of orbiting space stations, which are the basis for a major expansion into zero-g manufacturing.

THELOI

POLITICAL DESIGNATION: INDEPENDENT STAR SYSTEM
HABITABLE PLANETS: TWO
GOVERNING PLANET: THELOI
PRIMARY INDUSTRY: TRADING
ENVIRONMENT: CLASS G

Theloi is a mid-level merchant world which functions as hub of commerce. Few businesses actually manufacture product in Theloi, due to the system's lack of raw materials. Its location between several more productive systems, however, makes it an excellent clearing house for several different industries.

PONY GIRL

"Kismet," Acorna murmured,
staring up at the vid screen in the middle
of the viewing lounge. "'It was thus fated.'"
Or so Calum told her that was what the space station's
name meant. She had plenty of time to muse about
meanings and ancient languages. She could be aboard
Kismet for months. The spectroanalysis of the cluster
of nearby stars had looked promising. The satellites
of one or more of them might contain some of the
trace elements that had made up her infant escape pod.
One of them might even be her home. In spite of her
protestations that she ought to be part of any primary
exploration, her friends had left her behind.
Too dangerous to risk her, Gill had said.

BY JODY LYNN NYE
ILLUSTRATED BY JOHN RIDGWAY

She had protested, of course, but Calum had said, inarguably, "And what will we tell all the children if we lose you in a stupid accident while tapping asteroids?"

That had been the only argument that worked with Acorna, as all of them knew. She had still insisted on coming this far with them, wanting to be nearby if they found anything. But she missed her friends already.

In the meantime, she had been installed in a nice suite at the expense of Mr. Li and Uncle Hafiz Harakamian of House Harakamian. Uncle Hafiz himself was expected within the month. He had interests here, and some clients for whom this was a useful and very private conference center. She would be glad to see him.

On the screen, beautiful, liquid-eyed animals bounded forward, almost side by side, silky manes flying. Small humans in colorful, fluttering costumes clung to their backs, bobbing to the rhythm of their run. A man's voice narrated the spectacle, droning on in a strange, nasal monotone that Acorna could not understand.

Around her in the lounge, groups of richly garbed men and women sat behind private glass screens. More stood or sat in the common area, leaving nowhere for her to sit. She preferred to stand, anyhow. Her two-toed feet found a comfortable and secure base in the spongy but durable floor padding. The most interesting thing about the floor was that it made no noise at all when she walked. She would have to research the composition for its application on Maganos Moon Base.

The haven she operated for the children she'd freed from slave labor on Kezdet was well-established now, and she finally had an opportunity to go away. Not that it hadn't been a wrench to leave behind her beloved charges, but there were children here, she thought, as one scampered by her and disappeared through the door, if she could only get to meet some of them. She was glad to see these youngsters were well fed, and she never saw signs of physical abuse.

What odd fashions they wore on this station. She'd never seen anything quite like them. The boy was clad in soft, gold silk pantaloons, a dark crimson velvet jacket with a standup collar richly embroidered on sleeves, neck and front with gold, and a short, cylindrical cap with a high, red, cut-out crest in the shape of a heart.

Another child, this one a girl with beautiful high cheekbones and long eyelashes, dressed all in royal blue decorated with a crest shaped like a lion, came barreling out of yet another corridor but paused when she saw the tall lady in white standing by the vid monitor. Acorna smiled and dropped to her knees to beckon the child to her, but the girl's pause had been only momentary. Gawking, the little one backed away and ran in another direction. She didn't smile. Acorna sighed and rose to her feet.

"Give them time," Calum had said, when they'd landed on Kismet a few hours before. "They've never seen anything like you."

The children of Kezdet had been suspicious and fearful at first, too. Acorna counted upon the curiosity of the young to bring them to her in time. She was eager to talk to healthy, well brought up children, to hear how their lives differed from those of her wards, perhaps bring them new games or songs or e-beam-pals. She also admired their style of dress, which would flatter her leggy figure, but naturally, she would do without the hat. A horn was quite enough ornament for any head.

She turned back to the screen. The animals had stopped running, and a very small man in black and white was accepting a trophy from a woman in an embroidered jacket and crested hat. The beast behind them tossed its head and blew. How lovely it was.

"Is the honored lady interested in the transmission?"

A man in sage green and black had appeared at her side.

"Yes," she said. "I am curious. What was it?"

"A horse race," he said with obvious pride. "You are a guest of the station? You must be a mandarin, if you will excuse my boldness in observing so. You may, of course, place wagers if you choose. There are many such spectacles provided for the amusement of the guests, but the horse race, run every day at 1600, is the best attended. I, Kwan, will provide you with a betting monitor so you may keep track of your transactions, exchange odds with other interested persons both in person and by transmission and input your winnings, for surely such a lovely lady will win."

Acorna had had a brief but intensive lesson from Uncle Hafiz in how to calculate odds, for which she had a tremendous and suprising aptitude. She'd made some further study of the art when she had time. Her three guardians, Rafik in particular, had insisted that she had such advantages in her education and analytical ability that it was not fair for her to gamble against mere humans.

"I think not," she said, "but may I still watch?"

"If you like," Kwan said, his interest cooling visibly with no prospect of commissions.

One of the glass pods opened, and a child, in bright green and a feather-shaped crest, emerged. Perhaps he was coming out to play. Acorna turned to greet him.

"And hurry up about it!" a voice behind him barked. The child fled, not even stopping to look up at her.

Acorna saw the same driven expression on his face as she had on the beasts on the screen. The little ones she had seen were all racing somewhere and not of their own volition.

"Where do these children play?" she asked Kwan.

"Play?" he asked blankly. "The children of the mandarins play in the apartments of their parents."

"Are they going home, then?" Acorna asked, looking at the door through which the child in green had gone.

"*Those* are not their children," Kwan said, with a sniff.

On the screen, a red flash erupted. Another spectacle had begun. A cluster of small spaceships pulled away from a docking wheel and flew out and away from each other. White flashes began to break out on the hulls of several of the craft, and the narrator's voice droned on.

"Kwan!" a voice shouted from one of the glass chambers.

"Your pardon," Kwan said, and pattered away. Acorna left the viewing lounge to find her suite on level seven.

Anything over the size of a pallet was palatial after the cramped accomodations on Maganos, but the apartment she had been assigned was almost on the order of real estate. Her belongings had been placed in the largest bedchamber, which gave onto a splendid bath. Smaller rooms had been set aside for her former guardians, when they returned, and a suite-within-a-suite for Uncle Hafiz. On the dining table was a basket of fresh greens and fruit. Somewhere in the basket handle was a holochip, for hovering over the gift were the words WITH THE COMPLIMENTS OF THE MANAGE-MENT. Acorna munched some of the greens, wishing the others were there to share with her.

Kismet, said the brochure on the lounge table, had seventeen levels, each uniquely decorated and maintained to the highest standard. Acorna went on an exploration of the station. Like her suite, it was vast, beautifully designed, well-polished, and well kept. The gold ornamentation on the walls was carefully rounded so that no injuries would be sustained if the station went into zero-g. Lifts were available at every fifth arc of the rings, and there were moving sidewalks in between so one could ride rather than walk. Acorna preferred to walk.

She heard shouting up ahead. Such loud noises were so alien to the quiet of Kismet that she broke into a run to see what had happened. The lift doors were open, and dangling cables showed inside. Someone had been injured, for a cluster of people were kneeling on the ground near the doors.

"It just fell down on me," a man's weak voice said from the midst of the cluster.

Acorna could almost feel his pain through the air. She brushed everyone aside to get to him.

"Are you a doctor?" someone asked.

"A healer. Please give us room."

A large man pushed between them and the crowd and stood urging everyone back while Acorna examined the young man. He got his first good look at her; eyes traveled up to her horn, down her face to her long nose.

"Oh, please go away," he said, with wide eyes, even though his face was pale and drawn.

"You need help," she said. She inspected the wounds in his chest and arm. They were dirty where the cable had struck them. They could be infected. She felt the sweat spring up on the surface of her horn, and while the young man tried to push her away, gently rubbed the horn on his injuries. The healing was instantaneous, and when Acorna raised her head, the young man looked astonished. There was one more wound, on his thigh near the knee. Acorna bent almost with her head on his lap to touch that gash. When she looked up, he was scarlet with embarrassment.

"Ship's doctor, coming through," a hearty voice said. Acorna backed off to give him room. "What's all the fuss about? This man's fine."

Acorna slipped away into the growing crowd. The young man obviously didn't want to tell what she had done, but she didn't know why healing him would embarrass him so much.

⛊

In the restaurant, she was placed at a small table by herself, but a plump woman sitting with a man and their four children raised a hand and beckoned to her.

"Come and sit with us, my dear," she said. "Don't eat alone."

"Thank you," Acorna said.

The restaurant, like everything else on Kismet, was opulent but shipshape. Tables were of the finest wood and brass but bolted very discreetly to the floor. The chairs had magnets in their feet, making them heavy but mobile.

"I'm curious about your looks, my dear," the mother said. "You resemble an ancient symbol of my family's house."

"I have heard of the ki-lin," Acorna said. "But I do not know if we are related." She explained how three space miners had found her floating in a lifepod as an infant, and what little was known or had been deduced of her origins. The family was fascinated. "I am likely to be staying here for some time, until my friends arrive."

"We are in the midst of a six-week stay," Song Flower said. "Please, do visit with us as much as you can."

"I would love to," Acorna said, touched by Song Flower's maternal kindness. "I admire the style of clothes you wear. Where may I find some like that?"

"Oh, ask Kwan," the woman said, flicking a fan out of her sleeve and cooling her face with it even though the room was cool. "We depend upon him for everything. He will get you the best tailor. There is also plenty of shopping in levels one and seventeen, top and bottom, so you have views of the stars while you browse."

"It sounds very lovely there," Acorna said.

She spent the next day touring the station with Song Flower's children, who happily dragged her to all their favorite places. The youngest, Blue-eyed Cat, wanted to go back again and again to his favorite game arcade, but the other three were somewhat better hosts, taking her to places of general interest. At one point in the top shopping district, she thought she saw the young man she had healed, talking in low tones with a hefty woman in yellow silk. He nodded toward her when he saw her. Acorna thought he meant to acknowledge her, but when she started toward him, he turned away.

The invaluable Kwan had arranged an appointment for her with Dogtooth Violet, a tailor on 17, who measured her, clicking her tongue all the time. By the time they came back, she had a mandarin's coat and trousers of white silk picked out with blue embroidery and silver braid.

"Beautiful," Banded Eel said, shaking his head. "Mother will be jealous."

"Then she will commission one like it!" Blue-eyed Cat shouted gleefully.

Over the tannoy came the staccato tune of a bugle, followed by a bouncy little piece of music. If Acorna strained, she could hear words.

"Pony boy, pony boy, won't you be my pony boy…"

"That's the call to the post," said Young Lion, the eldest boy. "We have to go home. Mama likes us to be back in the apartment when she is betting."

"Then I will see you at dinner," Acorna said. "I would like to go and watch the horse race."

The main viewing room filled up fast. People came at the run to stand around the main viewer, their betting monitors in hand.

"Kwan," Acorna said, as he came by, "what became of the man who was injured in the elevator accident?"

"There was no accident," Kwan said, under his breath. "Man fine. All equipment fine."

"But…"

"They give him money to shut up, fix all, all fine. Too many accidents are bad for business," Kwan said hastily, and turned away. "Honored sirs and madams, the trifecta begins!" he shouted, trying to fit his favorite clients in at the best vantage points to watch.

The three heats were run, each featuring ten different horses. Acorna remembered Uncle Hafiz's lecture on trifecta betting. His advice had been to nobble the favorite and bet on the underdog.

Almost all of the participants looked discontented at the end of the third race. One young woman tipped her hands up and let her betting monitor fall to the floor. One man wearing an expression of extreme frustration took the hat off the child beside him and ripped the crest off. He said something sharp, and the child went over to a gray-haired woman lounging on a couch, who patted his arm. One young man was jubilant, jumping up and down and thrusting his little betting monitor at anyone who didn't move away quickly enough.

"Why are so many people interested in this particular contest?" Acorna asked the people nearby. "There are races and matches going on all day."

"Because it's real," a young woman in blue said. "Some of the other contests are only computer simulations or virtual reality contests, and the rest of them are vids beamed in from remote sites. But the horses are here on the station."

"It means the outcome can't be faked," one of the matrons said, fluttering her fan. "There have been frauds in the past."

"The horses are here?" Acorna asked. "That looked like a planet-side sky."

"Only the best for the racing animals," the first young woman said, with pride. "They are well-treated. You should go and see for yourself."

Acorna was delighted. "I will."

The stables filled the whole of level eight. Acorna visited the barns, where the horses leaned their lovely heads out over the half doors, begging for a pat or a scratch. They were even more beautiful than on the screen. Acorna adored their satiny coats and their delicate hooves that were not unlike her own long, square-tipped hands and feet.

The jockeys, none of whom stood taller than mid-chest to her, were happy to talk about their work and their beloved animals.

"They give us everything," said Varn Dosset, the stable manager. "We have our own auxiliary generator. We even have pasturage around the track. Come and see."

The field was surrounded by ceramic walls, but the artificial sky above was blue. Acorna breathed the smell of sweet grass, and for a moment, she felt as if she was planet-side again.

The track was turf, too. A crew worked to replace grass thrown up by the horses' hooves during the races. Acorna was tempted by the concept of a long run on the green expanse.

"May I?" she asked Dosset.

He grinned. "Of course, if you want."

Acorna squeezed between the fence rails and stood for a moment in the middle of the track, intoxicated by the heady smells of leather, wood, sweat, sour horse urine, sweet grass, instead of the aseptic smells of a space station. She broke into a trot, the soft silk of her trouser legs brushing in velvet rhythm. She ran faster, letting her mane stream back behind her. One revolution, two. As she passed them for the third time, she heard the jockeys on the sideline burst into song,

"Pony girl, pony girl, won't you be our pony girl…"

The singers broke into laughter. Acorna slowed to a walk and came over to laugh with them.

"I've enjoyed myself," she said. "I'm very grateful. May I come back?"

"Any time," they said.

She walked back to the lift station. The corridors were dark except for ceiling safety lights at intervals and a light over each door. She passed by one that bore the interplanetary symbol for danger. The roar beyond it sounded like a mass waste processor. Unusual to see a maintenance door in a main walkway on Kismet, but the stable folk undoubtedly needed easy access to dispose of stable litter. Across from it, at the edge of the next shadow, she saw a burst of green on the floor. It looked like a discarded garment. Acorna went closer. It was the little boy from the betting lounge, sitting all alone, hugging his knees.

He stared up at her, then huddled into himself more miserably than ever. His woeful face turned Acorna's kind heart upside down. She sat down beside him on the dusty floor and gathered him into her lap. He resisted for a moment, then cuddled against her, trembling.

"What's your name, sweetheart?" she asked.

"Birch Leaf," he said, in a very tiny voice.

"What a nice name. I am Acorna, Birch Leaf. What's the matter?" she asked.

"I have to walk into the fire," he said, "and I'm scared."

"What?" she asked. "That? The incinerator?"

He nodded.

"I have no place to go," he told her. "My employer has fired me. No one will feed me. I haven't saved enough to go away, and I must clear off the station."

His dark eyes were full of tears. "I asked the jockeys, but they do not have work for me. No one else has a job. I must clear off the station."

"What about your parents?" Acorna asked.

"They are on Yukian. They sent me here with Sir and Madam. They do not want me anymore." He looked at the door, and Acorna shuddered.

"Well, you will not walk into any fire," she said, lifting him up. "I have plenty of room. You will stay with me." If nothing else, she could arrange to bring him back to Maganos when she left.

~❦~

She went to the viewing lounge to talk to the family who had employed him. At the edge of their glass cage hovered a little girl in purple who now wore the feather-shaped crest. She must have known the fate of her predecessor, for she was pathetically eager to please.

"Why did you treat that child as you did?" Acorna asked.

112

"He was inefficient," the man said, flicking his plump fingers over the tiles on the gaming board. The half dozen people around the table looked bored. "I let him go."

"I have taken him in," Acorna said.

"I didn't know he was still alive," the man said, although his flat face barely changed expression. "You're welcome to him. I bought another, as you see. Excuse us, we have a game going." He stood up, urged Acorna backward by simply walking toward her, and shut the glass door on her. Acorna rounded upon Kwan, who was hovering nearby.

"Do these people *own* these children?" she demanded. "They are slaves?"

"Yes, of course they own them," Kwan said, impatiently, but she got an impression of hidden anger. "Not slaves. Property. Assets. Sometimes they trade them, collect them. You want one? Cost you four hundred, maybe, for a good one."

"I do not!"

Acorna was furious. When these callous people tired of their purchase, the unwanted possession was expected to throw itself away, tidy itself into a disposer.

She marched back into the glass cubicle. The group looked up, startled at the invasion. She pointed to the little girl.

"Sell me this one, too," Acorna said. "I don't want what nearly happened to Birch Leaf to happen to her." She could afford it; both Uncle Hafiz and Delszaki Li would back such a good cause with their considerable assets.

"No, of course, I will not," the man said, looking irritated. "I need her. Step aside. She has to register my bet. Move!" he shouted at the girl, who had hesitated for one moment, then fled.

"With all the electronic equipment at your disposal —with all the mechanical devices," Acorna asked, "why do you use children as carriers?"

"An old custom," the man said, with a slight smile, and his companions nodded. "They are allowed to buy themselves back if they choose."

"What with?" Acorna demanded.

The men and women shrugged, uninterested in where their messengers found a fortune. "Some do," one woman volunteered.

"It's a shameful practice," Acorna said. "They should grow up, have a decent education and loving homes." She had offered this argument before, on Kezdet, to the same kind of deaf ears and had had to take action on her own. "May I offer you a proposition? I will pay four hundred apiece for those children, all of them, if you switch to a mechanical system of placing your bets. I am a ward of House Harakamian. They will engineer the finest system for you, to your satisfaction."

"No!" they protested. "We like things the way they are," one woman said, clutching her game tiles as if they represented the status quo.

"I will offer you a counter-proposition," said the man who had owned Birch Leaf. "We won't sell them to you, but you can win them from us. Buying and selling is for peasants and merchants. Gambling is our sport. Put up your money, and we'll see whom Fate favors."

"Done," Acorna said and marched out.

Kwan was happy to fit her out with a betting monitor. He demonstrated how to use the peripheral slot for the minute disk that recorded her bets for the betting clerk and where she would insert a disk to deduct or add to the total of her bank.

"And your initial stake?" he asked.

Acorna entered a sum that made Kwan's eyebrows rise into the brim of his cap.

&⚜&

Song Flower was puzzled over why Acorna was interested in the bet-children. "It is not as if they were born to you," she said at dinner that evening.

"It should not be necessary that they are born to me," Acorna said, patiently, for Song Flower had been kind to her. Acorna had been further horrified to learn that the bet-children couldn't read or write. They knew numbers; house sigils of the mandarin families; symbols of each of the participants in the contests, whether horse, jockey, wrestler, starship, or chess player; and ship safety symbols; but that was all. They owned nothing, not even their garments, and slept wherever their employers had a square meter of empty space. "They are children, like your own. Each of them should have a loving family and a good education, so they can grow up to be good fathers and mothers themselves."

"Grow up?" Song Flower said, even more perplexed. Her fan flicked open and quivered. "Bet-children never grow up."

Acorna investigated and found that it was true. The suicide rate was almost total. A child could be dismissed on a whim. They were cut off immediately from the amenities of the station for which their employer had been paying. Almost all of them walked into the disposer room as the fastest and most certain form of death. Everywhere else was patrolled, and if a suicide made a mess somewhere in the ship and didn't succeed in dying, the former sponsor berated them angrily. The children were in despair. It was serve or die.

Acorna began to wager on all kinds of contests and spectacles, from wrestling down to cockroach races. She lost money at first, but gained seven children in the first week in lucky bets. The management of Kismet was persuaded to allow them to occupy empty cabins in dormitory fashion, and Acorna footed the bills for their upkeep and board. Acorna ascertained that there were enough empty cabins to take the number of servant children six times over.

She lost most of her wagers, until Kwan took her aside under pretense of handing her a betting chip for her monitor.

"Don't waste time on trivia," he said. "Avoid strict matters of chance." He showed her a list of spaceship battles, chess matches, planetary elections, and of course, the horse races, and gave her volumes of back data on past wins and losses. Acorna studied it all and started to make more intelligent wagers. And began to win more. When the bets were large, she spread them out among several other bettors. When they did not have a servant to put up against her cash wager, they paid off in cash. Her bank balance grew steadily.

❧✿☙

A small group of men and women were waiting for Acorna outside her suite. By their dress, most of them were merchants, but some were mandarins. "Lady, may we speak to you?" asked the merchant woman at their head, twining her hands together nervously. Acorna nodded, wondering if this was a delegation to ask her to stop her plan to win the bet-children's freedom. Word certainly had spread fast. "Lady, we hear you have done a divine healing."

"Not divine," Acorna said. "It is a natural process."

"It could not be," the woman said, and her eyes were hopeful. "No scars left behind, no pain—great Goddess, we come to ask humbly if we may worship at your feet."

"I am not a goddess," Acorna protested. "I am only Acorna."

The others smiled and nodded to one another, as if this was exactly what they expected her to say.

"The Eternal Mother come again," whispered a young man with wide, blue eyes.

"We will be satisfied if you will only walk among us and spread your blessing, so we may share it," said the spokeswoman.

That sounded very much like what she would do anyway, Acorna thought.

"Very well," she said.

From then on, she had one or more of the adherents of the Eternal Mother trailing behind her everywhere at a respectful distance. They brought her a sick teenager, whom Acorna healed easily with the application of her horn. The cure only increased her stock among them. Although they treated her with divine courtesy and immense respect, their ubiquitous presence quickly became a nuisance. Before long, she forbade them to follow her into certain places, especially down to the track.

Level eight was her favorite place on Kismet. Escaping from her train of worshipers, she planted her back against the door of the lift, enjoying the quiet and the mix of scents in the air.

Acorna spent enough time with the jockeys to learn a lot about their steeds. The way the skin indented between the muscles of their haunches told her which beast would run the fastest. The subtleties of shape of their delicate legs suggested which one might turn an ankle on the turf, all other things being equal. And her judgement improved beyond human standards.

Acorna continued to win. A lucky combination in the daily double of spaceship races in the middle of the third week put her thirteen children to the good. Few were left in service. The little ones began to strut confidently around the station before their former employers, who were upset at having to deliver their own bets. Song Flower, a convert to Acorna's way of thinking, allowed friends to employ her four children as runners.

Acorna stood in the center of the viewing lounge, collecting disks and recording them as quickly as she could. Fate favored her today. The faces of the children around her were radiant with hope.

"Win me next," whispered the little girl in purple.

"I will try," Acorna promised.

Suddenly, the viewscreen and all the wall lights went out.

"Hey!" someone shouted. Bright white spotlights came on over the passageways, casting confused shadows everywhere.

"What happened?" Acorna asked.

"Attention, please!" the tannoy announced, cutting through the uproar. "There has been a slight mishap. Will everyone please proceed at once to level eight? There is nothing to worry about. Thank you."

"Mishap?" a deep voice demanded.

"Why level eight?" someone asked.

Acorna remembered. "They have their own generator."

"Is the life support out?" a woman screamed.

"Another accident!" came Kwan's voice at her elbow. "Just like the lift. I knew this would happen one day, and this time they won't be able to cover it up. Thousands of people on this station will all die."

Suddenly the huge room felt cold. Some of the children began to cry.

"Come along," Acorna said, grabbing two of the nearest by their hands. "No one will die. We're going to see the horses. Follow me!"

"Follow the lady!"

The boys and girls hurried after her. In the glare of the safety lights, Acorna saw adults nervously joining the file. Some were weeping, but she'd forestalled most of the hysteria by acting quickly. The temperature continued to drop precipitously.

The lifts were not functioning, so Acorna opened the access stairs without hesitation and clattered down the metal steps with her charges. No silent padding here.

At level eight, she had to step aside while strong men broke the safety lock on the access door. Her followers streamed into the corridor, and she led them toward the stables, where it was still warm.

"We heard the announcement," Dosset said, meeting them near the barns. "You're welcome, but I don't know how long our generator will last, having to process for all these people."

"It stinks down here," a woman complained.

"Would you rather not breathe at all?" a man rasped.

Even though there was an artificial blue sky above, the mandarins, in their silks, huddled together in fear, speculating as to what was happening above. The staff had come down, too, and were in their own frightened knot. Acorna went back and forth, followed by her adherents, offering cheer and hope. She did not want to tell them about her purifying abilities, hoping they wouldn't be needed.

But they were. In only a few hours, the air began to feel heavy. Some of the employees near the perimeter of the pasture looked woozy, swaying on their feet. Varn Dosset brought the horses in and shut off support to all parts of the level except the pasture to save fuel. That helped for a while.

Kwan kept in touch with the repair crew and passed on the news that they were working as fast as they could to bring the main generator back on line. He did not say what the fault was, but Acorna guessed from the look in his eyes that his speculation had been correct.

Acorna felt the sweat begin to form on her horn. The air was becoming foul.

"Move together, everyone," she urged. "It's getting cold. We will keep warm together."

The mandarins were unhappy at having to nestle close to the support staff, and particularly the horses, but they complied. Acorna held her head and horn as high as she could and hoped her strength would hold out long enough. She circulated around and through the crowd over and over, willing the sweet air to spread out to the throng around her, two thousand people and forty horses.

It seemed as if she held that pose for an eon. People chatted to one another in low voices. The children, mandarin and servant, played together on the grass. They all stopped, as a deep rumble vibrated through the floor and the walls.

"The ventilator has just kicked back on," Kwan exclaimed. "It was off! But the air is still good here. How?"

"It's her," the children said, pointing at Acorna. "The clean air follows her."

"She is the Great Mother come again!" her worshipers insisted, feeling free at last to reveal her secret. A murmur swept through the crowd. Some recoiled from Acorna as if she was a monster, but some pressed closer. "She purifies all that she touches."

"You've saved us all," Dosset said, shaking her hand vigorously. "Us and our horses. I'm grateful."

"Lady, how can we repay you?" some of the others asked.

"Life for life," Acorna said, after a moment's thought. "I want you to adopt the bet-children."

"What?" some demanded, outraged, forgetting their near brush with death.

"That's my condition. You will treat them as your own. Love them, teach them, give them discipline and affection. Never again should they fear starvation or be forced into suicide. And you will buy no more, ever."

"Is that all?" a man asked dubiously.

"It is everything," Acorna said.

"I shall take four more," Song Flower said at once. "How about the rest of you?"

"I will, too," Dosset said. "She saved our horses. It's the least I can do."

"Have I missed today's race?" asked a familiar voice. Acorna turned to see Hafiz Harakamian of House Harakamian striding toward her. He enveloped her in a hug of swirling silk robes. "Ah, I see I have. Our engineers have assisted the station's to correct the little hiccup in service. It's quite nice up there, now. My, what has happened here to produce such a diversity of glum and happy faces?"

"Come and I will tell you, Uncle Hafiz." Acorna pulled him away from the crowd. The gamblers were still licking their wounds and pondering the sudden parenthood that had been bestowed upon them, the followers of the Great Mother were trying to figure out the true meaning of Acorna's words and it was just beginning to dawn upon the children that they were property no longer. Acorna and Hafiz had not quite reached the lifts when a shrill whoop went up.

Uncle Hafiz listened to her story in his patient way, leaning back in a deep chair with his fingers tented together. Acorna showed him the gambling monitor and the sum displayed on its little screen.

"I see," he said. "You have earned House Harakamian a fat commission in new equipment. Good. And of their total assets, this represents what percentage?"

Acorna frowned. "A hundred percent of the children's lives, Uncle. What becomes of the gamblers after this is not my concern."

Hafiz sighed gustily, but his eyes were twinkling. He sat up and tapped her on the knee.

"Darling child, have I taught you no better than that? Why do they still have their shirts?"

ACORNA'S SERUM

Acorna stepped through the entrance
tunnel and immediately began searching
for Professor Cormac. Although she was
dressed in drab, shapeless clothes, with
sunglasses and a scarf around her head,
her appearance was still different enough to
cause questioning stares from her fellow travelers.
Of course, Acorna understood how unique she was among
humans who had never seen anyone quite like her before, but
their curiosity still made her uncomfortable.

After retrieving their credentials from the customs
inspector, Pal Kendoro came up beside Acorna.
"I believe that's Professor Cormac over there," he said.

❧ BY ROMAN A. RANIERI ❧
ILLUSTRATIONS BY JOHN RIDGEWAY

A tall, stocky man with gray hair waved to get her attention as he approached. Acorna headed toward him.

"I'm Professor Cormac," he said, extending his hand. "I'm very happy to meet you. I hope your flight wasn't too tiring."

"It was not very comfortable. Will it take long to get to the Universal Medical Institute?"

"Less than an hour. U.M.I. is located near Tullamore." Cormac reached for Pal's hand. "And you must be Mr. Kendoro. My old friend, Delszaki Li, speaks very highly of you."

"Mr. Li also speaks highly of you, Professor. He sends his warmest regards and trusts you will assure Acorna's comfort and security during her stay at the Institute," replied Pal.

"Certainly. I have already made all the security arrangements that Delszaki suggested. Acorna will be as safe and comfortable as possible. If you have all your luggage, we can go outside to my vehicle and get started."

"I have everything I need," said Acorna, nodding to the small duffle bag slung over her shoulder.

Professor Cormac gave her a dubious look. "I've never seen any female travel so lightly before."

"Why carry more than I need?" she replied.

"Eh, yes, quite right. Let's be on our way."

"Are you positive you don't want me to come along, Acorna?" asked Pal, a trace of hopefulness in his tone.

"It will take several weeks to complete the various business dealings Mr. Li gave you. You will never finish everything if you come with me. Do not worry. I'll be safe with Professor Cormac."

Pal nodded reluctantly. "Okay. But we'll keep in contact on a regular schedule. I want to know that you're all right."

Acorna hugged Pal and lightly kissed his cheek. "If I need you, I'll call. As for now, we both have work to do, and we should get started."

Acorna and Cormac left the transport terminal, and soon they were skimming smoothly along the Irish countryside in the professor's vehicle. Acorna gazed through the window at the lush green grass and the multicolored leaves of the autumn trees. She recognized farm crops and other edible vegetation on either side of the roadway, and her stomach growled hungrily. The salad the flight attendant had served her had been bland and unappetizing.

"We're all very honored at U.M.I. that you've agreed to help us," said Professor Cormac, breaking the silence.

"I was raised by humans. If I can help stop this plague, then I could not refuse your invitation. But you must understand that my abilities might not be the answer you need."

"Yes, of course. In medical research there are never any guarantees. But at the moment, we're at a standstill. Even if you can only point us in a new direction, it will be an immense help."

"I will do my best. Please tell me more about the plague," said Acorna, focusing her full attention on Cormac.

"For lack of a better term, we've dubbed it the Activ virus. It attacks the DNA polymerase enzymes in all life forms we've tested thus far; humans, animals, insects, everything. Since its first appearance, seven months ago, the virus has been completely lethal. Not one patient has survived more than three weeks. At this point, we must assume that even you are susceptible to it. Every precaution will be taken to assure your protection while you assist us."

"My horn protects me from disease and poison alike," said Acorna.

"I'm sure it does. Nevertheless, it's standard procedure to minimize the risks as much as possible."

Acorna again turned her attention to the passing scenery. "Earth is a very beautiful planet. Is that why the Institute was located here?" she asked.

Professor Cormac chuckled. "No, I'm afraid the reasons were far from aesthetic. Since Earth has the oldest history of all the inhabited planets, we also have the oldest and most complete archives of medical knowledge. Now, doctors and scientists from all nations and planets come here to study and conduct research at U.M.I. Every healing practice in the galaxy from Acupuncture to Zenoemersion is studied and taught here."

"Beauty can heal," said Acorna, admiring a valley of golden grain waving hypnotically in the cool afternoon breezes.

"Yes. Indeed it can," replied Cormac, smiling.

The remainder of the trip passed in silence. Cormac felt a sense of pride at Acorna's enjoyment of his native Irish landscapes and refrained from interrupting her concentration with technical data and theories about the virus. There would be plenty of time for business after she was comfortably settled in at U.M.I.

Twin stone columns on either side of a wide driveway marked the entrance to the Institute. Atop each column was a bronze sculpture of the caduceus, a winged staff with two snakes coiled around it, the honored and ancient emblem of the medical profession.

"Would you like to freshen up and have a bite to eat before meeting Chairman Jablon and the other members of the research team?" asked Cormac.

"Yes, very much," replied Acorna. "Thank you for being so kind."

Cormac escorted her to one of the suites in the residents' wing of the Infectious Diseases Research Center. After showing her how to use her vid-terminal to order food from the commissary, he arranged to meet her again in two hours.

"You're our guest here at U.M.I. Please don't hesitate to ask for anything you might need."

"I look forward to meeting everyone later. Thank you again, Professor."

When she was alone, Acorna walked straight into the bedroom and flopped tiredly on the bed. For the hundredth time, she wondered if her decision to come here had been too hasty. She was confident in her ability to heal humans, even bring them back from death if necessary. But a virus that spread to thousands of new victims each day, could she really expect to do much good against something like that?

⟡

"Welcome to our facility, Miss Acorna. I am Chairman Jablon. Thank you for accepting our invitation." The man behind the huge wooden desk rose to his feet but did not approach Acorna. Although he was smiling, his hawk nose and beady eyes gave him a somewhat sinister appearance. Acorna moved to the front edge of the desk and extended her hand.

"And thank you for your generous hospitality, Chairman. I promise to do my best to help end the suffering and death caused by this virus."

"I'm sure you'll be a tremendous asset. Allow me to introduce the other members of the research team. This is Doctor Gustave Brooker, our geneticist. Doctor Mai Tatsuno, our microbiologist. Doctor Louis Teillo, our pathologist. And you've already met Professor Cormac, our doctor of internal medicine."

Acorna shook hands with each person as they were introduced. Gustave Brooker was a rotund man with a bald head and delicate hands which seemed too small for his body. Mai Tatsuno was short and slender with thick horn-rimmed glasses that magnified her dark eyes, giving her an owlish appearance. Louis Teillo flashed a dazzlingly handsome smile as he bowed to kiss Acorna's hand in the old continental fashion.

A few minutes later, the group left Chairman Jablon's office and headed for the laboratories. While they walked, Acorna listened intently as the doctors took turns describing how their particular fields of expertise contributed to the Activ virus research project.

When Acorna spoke, it was to ask pertinent and intelligent questions. The doctors exchanged approving glances, impressed by her remarkable understanding of medical concepts and terminology, knowledge she'd gained working among the sick and injured on Kezdet. What they had heard was true —Acorna possessed a healing talent so natural and intrinsic to her being, that it was almost pure instinct.

By the time they reached the labs, the doctors felt an optimism and enthusiasm that they hadn't been able to generate for weeks. Perhaps this amazing young woman really could help them find the way to stop Activ's deadly epidemic.

Acorna rubbed her eyes, then looked up at the clock on the opposite wall. It was forty minutes after midnight. She had been in the lab for nearly twelve hours. Although the doctors had urged her to leave with them when they quit for the night, Acorna had insisted on staying longer to finish reading the latest batch of test results. She was getting ready to go back to her suite when she heard the creak of the lab door being opened.

"Hello? Anyone in here?" called a young male voice.

"Yes. I am here. Can I help you?" replied Acorna.

A tall, thin teenager hesitantly peeked around the edge of the door. "I'm sorry if I disturbed you," he apologized. "I saw the lights from the corridor and thought maybe someone forgot to turn them off. The doctors usually don't work this late."

"No harm done. I'm Acorna. I have come to help with the virus research."

"Hi. I'm Peter Wilson. I'm Chairman Jablon's lab assistant. It's a real honor to meet you. The whole institute is talking about you."

121

"Why would everyone want to talk about me?"

"Are you kidding?" laughed Peter. "You're unique. Until now, there's never been anyone with your kind of healing powers. It's like magic."

"Not magic," said Acorna defensively. "I just do what is natural for me to do."

Peter was silent for a few moments, then nodded. "Yeah, I guess it's tough having all this attention focused on you. You'd probably appreciate it more if we'd all just treat you like a regular person. Right?"

Acorna smiled. "I would like that very much."

After a ten-minute walk to the resident's wing, Acorna and Peter were already on their way to becoming good friends. She liked the way he acknowledged that she was different, yet didn't gawk at her or ask the usual assortment of silly personal questions. He was willing to simply accept her.

"Well, I guess I'd better get back to my dorm. I have an anatomy report to finish by Tuesday. But I'll be assisting Chairman Jablon in the lab tomorrow afternoon, so I guess I'll see you then."

"I'll be there," said Acorna. "Thank you for making me feel more comfortable."

"You're very welcome. If I can be of any help, just ask. I've been a student here for three years now. I know where everything is."

"Good night, Peter. Have a restful sleep."

Two weeks of exhausting research had taken its toll on all the team members. Their initial glow of enthusiasm had quickly evaporated as repeated tests seemed to indicate that Acorna's healing functions could not be duplicated without her direct physical participation. Unless they found a way to create a reproducible serum from Acorna's horn, they'd have no hope of treating the thousands of infected people simultaneously, and it was impossible for Acorna to cure each person individually. The virus worked too rapidly for that.

One of the few bright spots for Acorna during the long days of frustrating tests and disappointing results was her new friendship with Peter Wilson. He seemed to know precisely when to interrupt her thoughts with an amusing story and when to remain quietly unobtrusive. Perhaps she could invite him to Kezdet sometime to meet her adopted family.

Acorna's thoughts were brought back to the present when Doctor Teillo handed her a vid-cube. "It still doesn't work," he sighed dejectedly. "Although touching the virus with your horn successfully kills the disease, the serums we've made from the bioptic tissue taken from your horn have almost no effect."

"I'm sorry I can't be more help. I've never given much thought to how my horn heals. I just know that it does."

"You've been marvelous, Acorna. We are the ones who are failing. Unless we identify those unknown elements in your physiology which are responsible for your healing abilities, we have no hope of manufacturing an effective serum from your tissue sample."

"We could try—"

Everyone was shocked into silence by the somber expression on Chairman Jablon's face as he entered the lab and slowly sat down in his accustomed seat. He looked around the room, confirming that all the members of the research team were present, and then he spoke. "I'm sorry to have to inform everyone that my assistant, Peter Wilson, committed suicide last night."

Doctor Tatsuno gasped, then removed her glasses and wiped at her eyes. Brooker, Teillo, and Cormac lowered their heads in stunned sadness.

"What has happened? What is suicide?" asked Acorna.

"Peter took his own life," said Cormac as gently as possible. "He's dead."

Acorna's jaw dropped open in disbelief for several moments. She could not believe that anyone would do something so senseless and self-destructive. Especially not Peter. He had been so cheerful and eager to help. What could have driven him to end his life? Acorna had to know.

"Take me to his body," she demanded. "I will bring him back and talk to him."

"I'm afraid that's not possible. Peter swallowed some Bellium isotopes. His body is now radioactive and must remain sealed in a quarantine container," said Chairman Jablon.

"It is not possible. I knew Peter. He was my friend. He would not kill himself."

"I'm sorry, Acorna. This is very upsetting for everyone. We all thought we knew Peter. But sometimes a person will keep their inner emotions hidden from others, even their friends."

"No! You're wrong," said Acorna angrily. "If you won't tell us the truth, then I will find out what happened."

"There will be a memorial service in the hospital chapel at ten tomorrow morning. The virus research is hereby suspended until after the service." Chairman Jablon rose from his chair. "I appreciate your feelings, Acorna. The death of a friend is always devastating, especially if it's in such a needless manner. You have my condolences."

Acorna nodded curtly, then gathered up her things and walked out of the lab.

❦

The memorial service was attended by the research team, the medical school faculty, and most of Peter Wilson's classmates. There was no coffin, only a large framed photograph on an easel surrounded with flowers.

In her mind, Acorna remembered every moment she had spent with Peter and replayed their conversations in her memory as accurately as she could recall them. She still could not believe he would kill himself. He was so dedicated to his studies and so enthusiastic about his future as a doctor. What could have made him give up everything he seemed to value?

That afternoon, Acorna entered Peter's dormitory and stopped the first student she saw.

"Excuse me. I need to visit the room that belonged to Peter Wilson."

"Oh, are you here to pack up his things?" asked the young man.

"No. We were working on the same project, and I need some of the notes he was reviewing."

"Okay. Follow me."

A few moments later, she was seated at Peter's small desk, attempting to find the password that would access his personal vid-files. She glanced around for some confirming clue to the troubled side of his nature that she had never known existed, but found nothing. The room was less than half the size of Acorna's suite in the resident's wing. The furnishings were plain and institutional. Peter had done nothing to personalize the space.

It took less than fifteen minutes for Acorna to access the files. Peter's password had been a simple mathematical progression of his birthday, his dorm room number, and his projected graduation date. She carefully scanned through his virus research notes. All of the various bits of information coincided with the data Acorna was familiar with, until she came to a reference to *Test 221 AV 051*. At first, she thought this must have been something the group was working on before she arrived, but the test number was too high for that. The first experiment conducted with Acorna's tissue sample had been designated *Test 221 AV 029*. *051* had to be less than a week ago. Why hadn't she been included in this experiment? She hadn't even been told it was being conducted.

Acorna decided to make a vid-cube copy of Peter's research files and examine them in more detail back at her suite. As the file directory scrolled up, she happened to notice her own name flash past. When the vid-cube copy was finished, curiosity brought her back to the Acorna file. What she found amazed her.

Peter had compiled an extensive album of interviews, articles, and photographs of Acorna. Although she disliked publicity and avoided it whenever possible, her rescue of the children on Kezdet had made her something of a celebrity to freedom-loving races on all planets.

Acorna felt a new sense of loss. Apparently, Peter's interest in her had been more than platonic friendship.

She picked up a holographic photo-cube of Peter from the bureau next to the bed. He was smiling, standing on a snow-covered mountain and holding a pair of long flattened sticks. "They must be some type of sporting apparatus," Acorna guessed. "I don't think this picture will be missed."

She slipped the photo-cube inside her tunic, then quietly left the dorm.

⟡

Three days following the memorial service, the research project had gotten more or less back on schedule. Chairman Jablon had already begun interviewing an assortment of students vying for the now vacant assistant's position.

Acorna knocked on the door to Professor Cormac's private office. After a short pause, Cormac opened the door. His face brightened instantly.

"What a pleasant surprise. Please come in, Acorna. How can I help you?"

"I am confused about something. Could you please tell me about *Test 221 AV 051?*"

"*51?* Isn't it covered in the research files?"

"No, Professor. I can't find any reference to it."

"Well, that's odd. All the virus test reports should be included in the main data bank. Please sit down while I check my own files."

Acorna seated herself in the thickly padded armchair facing the black lacquered desk that dominated the mid-sized office. The professor's expression changed from puzzlement to suspicion, then back again as he scanned through his files. Finally, he looked up at Acorna.

"This is really very strange. Are you positive that a *Test 221 AV 051* was actually conducted?"

"Yes. I found a reference to it in Peter Wilson's files. I believe he was working on it when he died."

"How did you access Wilson's files? It's against U.M.I. policy to tamper with someone's private records."

"I did not tamper with anything. I am investigating Peter's death," Acorna replied calmly.

Cormac's face softened. "Acorna, I'm aware that you and Peter had developed a close friendship. But that doesn't excuse your blatant disregard for Institute rules and regulations. Why can't you simply accept the unfortunate fact that Peter committed suicide?"

"Because I know he didn't. I'm positive that *Test 221 AV 051* had something to do with his death. Please help me find the truth. I can sense that you are a man of honor and integrity."

Cormac slowly shook his head. "You're talking to the wrong person, Acorna. I was the Chairman of U.M.I once, until I crossed paths with Chairman Jablon over experimentation regulations. Honor and integrity got me booted down here then, and I'm not going to risk what's left of my career on your hunch."

Acorna stood up. She reached across the desk and placed the palm of her hand against Cormac's cheek. "You will do what you know is right. A man like you has no other choice."

Since Chairman Jablon was the administrator of the Activ virus research project and answerable solely to the U.M.I. Board of Directors, Acorna felt certain that he had to know something about *Test 221 AV 051*. She was also certain that he would disavow any knowledge of that secret experiment if she asked him directly.

Late that night, when the only area of activity was the hospital building, Acorna stealthily crept along the hedge that bordered the western wall of the research lab offices. Chairman Jablon's suite was at the corner of the building, more than twenty feet beyond the end of the hedge. Acorna glanced around, making sure that she was alone in this section of the Institute's immense grounds, then she sprinted to the corner window.

She pulled a small case from the folds of her black robe, opened it and withdrew a slender metal object. Acorna smiled to herself. It was lucky that Calum, Gill, and Rafik were not aware of everything Uncle Hafiz had taught her.

The latch flipped up, the window hissed open, and Acorna climbed inside Jablon's private office so quickly that only someone with highly trained night-vision would have noticed even the slightest movement. She carefully turned the vid-monitor so that the glow of the screen would not be visible from either window.

From a different fold of her robe, Acorna withdrew another useful gadget Uncle Hafiz had loaned to her, in consideration of an unspecified favor she promised to repay sometime in the future, of course. She clamped the device onto the terminal and switched it on. Within seconds, Jablon's private, encoded files were scrolling up in easily-readable Basic Universal.

Acorna slowed the screen as the Activ virus files began to appear. She rapidly passed over the records she was familiar with, searching for *Test 221 AV 051*. It was here somewhere. She had never been more certain of anything in her life.

Then Acorna found it.

Her face only inches from the screen, she intently studied the report. When she finally reached Chairman Jablon's summary, Acorna was nearly overcome with rage and anguish.

Peter Wilson had selflessly agreed to be the first human test subject for the virus research program. Jablon and Doctor Brooker had somehow bribed or coerced Peter into allowing himself to be infected with Activ, then they had administered 10cc's of the most promising of the serums made from Acorna's tissue sample. When it became obvious that the serum was failing, the two doctors tried to cure him using every procedure known to science, but, of course, nothing had worked. Peter had died in agony, needlessly.

More infuriating than the stupidity of the experiment itself was the selfish negligence of Jablon and Brooker. If they had only brought Peter to her, Acorna could have saved him. But instead of seeking her help, they had let him die rather than admit what they had done. After he was dead, they had shoved some Bellium isotopes down his throat to prevent an autopsy.

Acorna quickly made a copy of the *051* report. There had to be some higher authority somewhere on this planet that would punish Jablon and Brooker for what they had done. She vowed to bring justice down upon these men.

She was nearly at the window when the office door banged open.

"I though I saw someone crawl in here," said Jablon, brandishing a laser gun in his right hand. "I suspected it was you."

"I know that you and Booker killed Peter."

"Peter understood the fact that sacrifices must be made in medical research. He volunteered for the experiment. He would not want his death to delay finding a cure for Activ while thousands of people die without hope. He would've been a great doctor."

"Yes, he would have been," said Acorna, her eyes narrowed to gleaming slits, "but you took all that away from him."

Before he could react, Acorna leaped. Her feet thudded solidly into Jablon's chest, knocking him back through the doorway into the corridor. As he struggled to regain his breath, she darted past him toward the building exit.

Acorna was much swifter than a normal human, but the highly polished floor provided her with very little traction. She knew all the lab doors would be locked at this hour of the night. Her only hope was to get out of the building.

She heard Jablon's pounding feet close behind. Desperation had given him a sudden burst of speed. In front of her, where the corridor made a left turn, was a window.

Acorna dove, tucking her knees up to her chest. Glass shattered, long slivers of it tearing ragged gashes in her robe. Acorna hit the soft grass tumbling like an acrobat. An instant later, she was up and running again.

Jablon was wheezing as he gingerly eased himself through the broken window. For a moment, he had a clear shot at Acorna, but he didn't take it. He was committed to stopping her, but not quite committed to killing her. There was only one person Acorna trusted in this place—Professor Cormac. She ran toward the resident's wing. Although winded, Jablon managed to stay within sight of Acorna. When he realized where she was going, he again rasied his gun.

Cormac was enjoying a rare, old classic film, *Die Hard*, on his vid-monitor when he heard someone hammering at the door of his suite. He rushed to the door and opened it, barely catching Acorna as she fell against him.

"What's wrong? Are you hurt?" he asked.

"Chairman Jablon is chasing me," she gasped. "He and Brooker used Peter for an unauthorized experiment. They killed him."

"Do you know what you're saying? What a serious charge you're making?"

"I have evidence. A copy of the test report here in

my robe. *Test 051*. I can prove it to you, but we must get away from here now. He's right behind me."

Acorna's terror convinced Cormac that something was terribly wrong. He stood to lock the door, but Jablon crashed through it and sent him sprawling. He quickly regained his footing and pulled Acorna behind him, defensively.

"Get away from her, Cormac," yelled Jablon, the gun trembling in his hand. "I'm not going to let her destroy my career."

"You really did this?" Cormac was stunned. "How could you jeopardize someone's life so recklessly? You knew those serums weren't ready for human testing."

"Thousands of people are dying from Activ every day. How long should we wait to help them? If the serum had worked, we'd all be heroes now. They'd be erecting statues of us on every planet at this very moment."

"You're insane, Jablon. There is no excuse for what you've done."

"Get the hell away from her," yelled Jablon. "This doesn't need to go any further. I'll give you whatever you want. Just don't let her destroy our work." Jablon leveled his pistol at Acorna.

"NO! I'm not going to let you harm her. For Christ's sake, you're supposed to be a doctor, not a murderer! Put down that gun, or you'll have to kill both of us."

Jablon stood frozen for what seemed like an eternity, then he dropped the gun and slowly sank to his knees, sobbing uncontrollably.

Cormac turned to Acorna and held her gently. "Are you all right?"

"Yes, Professor," she said with a weary smile. "Thanks to you."

Acorna and Cormac stood together at one of the huge transport terminal windows.

"I'm going to miss you," Cormac said. "You're a very special young woman."

"Thank you, Professor. I'm proud and happy to count you among my friends. I apologize for leaving U.M.I. before the project is completed, but the message from Kezdet sounded urgent."

"Don't worry, Acorna. We'll be able to continue the research with the tissue samples you so generously provided for us. I'm sure they will be the means by which we'll finally stop the Activ plague. And you can rest assured that with Jablon and Brooker safely imprisoned, no one at U.M.I. will ever again be placed in danger for the sake of research."

"I am quite sure of that. Especially with you in charge," said Acorna.

"What are you talking about?" Cormac asked.

"When I met with the Board of Directors, I suggested that you were the best person they could choose as the new Chairman. I was not surprised when they agreed unanimously. They're planning to announce the formal appointment tomorrow. I asked them to wait so I could be the one to tell you."

Cormac beamed. He hugged Acorna warmly as they heard the announcement that her flight was boarding, and Pal arrived with only seconds to spare.

"Thank you, my dear. You come back as soon as possible, you hear? There's much of my home that you haven't seen yet."

"You mean U.M.I.?" asked Acorna, puzzled.

"Of course not. I mean Ireland."

THE STORY OF KEZDET AND ITS DENIZENS REACHES FAR
HERE, THEN, ARE THE TALES OF THOSE WHOSE PATHS HAVE

ACORNA
THE UNICORN GIRL
BIOGR

BEFORE AND BEYOND THE BOOK YOU'VE NOW READ.
CROSSED WITH THAT OF THE SAVIOR FROM THE STARS.

APHIC

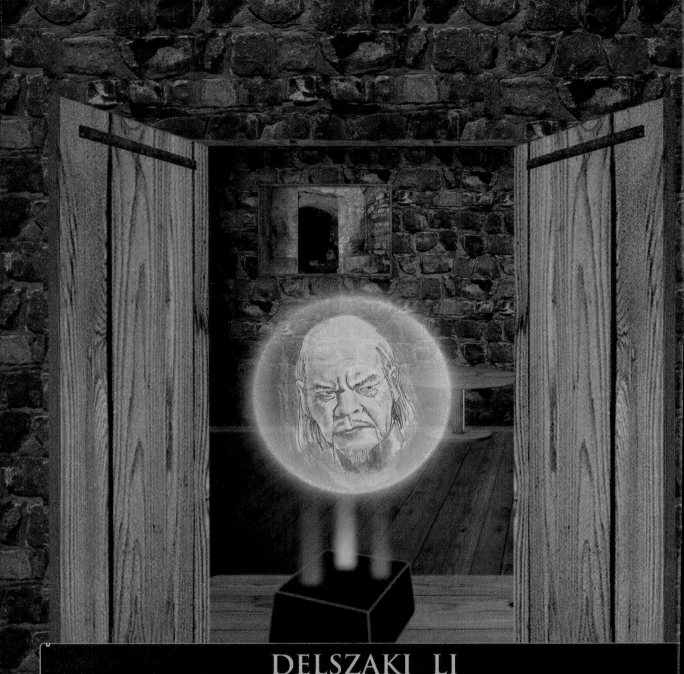

DELSZAKI LI

Height: 5'8" · Weight: 145 lbs · Hair: Black · Eyes: Black

Afflicted with a neuromuscular disease which renders his legs and right arm all but useless, Delszaki Li still succeeds in running the Li financial empire with his keen mind and commanding voice. Li runs his business on Kezdet without relying on child labor, a practice which has earned him many enemies on a world where children are routinely exploited. He is also a primary supporter of the Child Labor League, an illegal organization which works to end the slavelike employment of children that is so common on Kezdet. His Chinese ancestry exposed him to the legend of the Ki-Lin, a powerful unicorn whose presence is a harbinger of great changes for the better. He hopes Acorna will prove to be the Ki-Lin for Kezdet.

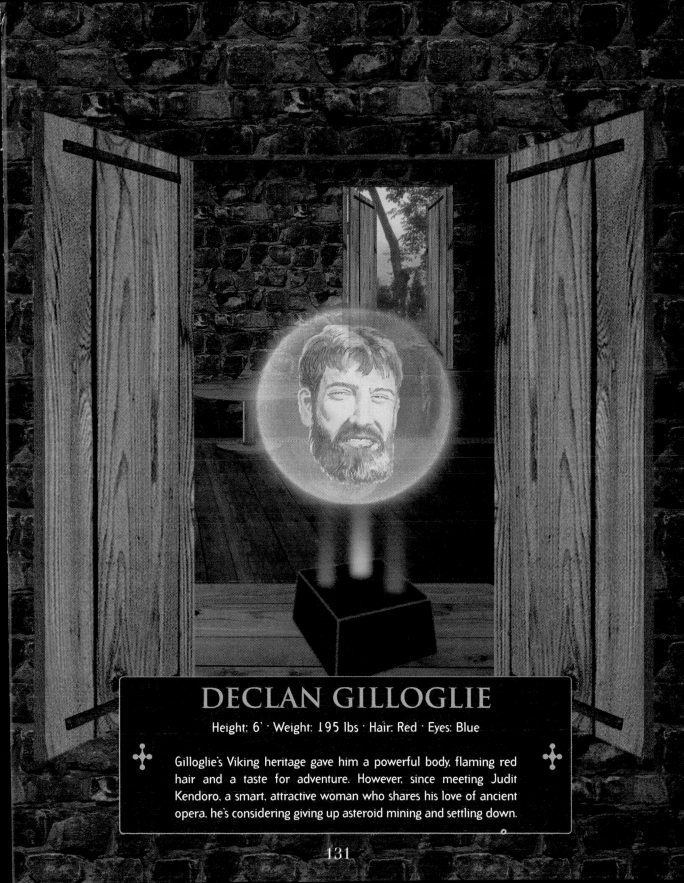

DECLAN GILLOGLIE

Height: 6' · Weight: 195 lbs · Hair: Red · Eyes: Blue

Gilloglie's Viking heritage gave him a powerful body, flaming red hair and a taste for adventure. However, since meeting Judit Kendoro, a smart, attractive woman who shares his love of ancient opera, he's considering giving up asteroid mining and settling down.

HAFIZ HARAKAMIAN

Height: 5'9" · Weight: 170 lbs
Hair: Black · Eyes: Black

Hafiz Harakamian is the most notorious merchant in known space. He is considered a master trader who is almost impossible to best in business negotiations. His habit of collecting unique things sparked his interest in Acorna, but he later gave up the idea when he realized that there are probably more like her on her home world. Instead, Hafiz took an interest in Rafik Nadezda, his nephew, and invited the boy to become his heir in place of his son, Tapha, who was unfit for the responsibility.

RAFIK
NADEZDA

Height: 5'10" · Weight: 180 lbs
Hair: Black · Eyes: Brown

Nadezda found Acorna's lifepod with his two partners, and later used his shrewd business sense to protect her. Rafik even out-negotiated his Uncle Hafiz Harakamian, a legendary merchant and deal-maker, impressing the man so much that he made his nephew heir to House Harakamian.

DIDI BADINI

Height: 5'9" · Weight: 150 lbs ·
Hair: Dk. Brown · Eyes: Dk. Brown

The title Didi, which means "big sister," applies only ironically to Didi Badini, who takes children from the mines of Kezdet and puts them to work in her houses of ill repute or "bonk-houses." Badini is well-known and well-feared by the indentured children of Kezdet. On the surface she is a beautiful, brown-skinned woman dressed luxuriously in the finest kameez and shalwar. But her eyes reveal her true nature with their cold, dark stare, as if Old Black himself was looking through them.

PAL KENDORO

Height: 5'10" · Weight: 180 lbs ·
Hair: Brown · Eyes: Brown

Pal works as Delszaki Li's personal assistant and is also the sister of Judit Kendoro. His sister's efforts away from Kezdet made it possible for Pal to complete his indenture in the child labor force and leave that hellish world behind him. He is a young, idealistic man and is active in the Child Labor League. Despite the obvious differences between their species, Pal is infatuated with Acorna and hopes they can build some kind of intimate relationship.